Best Wishes
Iris Glass

CHECKERED COURAGE

CHUCKWAGON RACING'S GLASS FAMILY

Glen Mikkelsen

JG
Johnson Gorman Publishers

The Publishers
Johnson Gorman Publishers
2003 – 35 Avenue SW
Calgary AB Canada T2T 2E2
info@jgbooks.com
www.jgbooks.com

Credits
Front cover photo courtesy of Paul and Carol Easton
Back cover photos courtesy of Paul and Carol Easton
Cover design by ArtPlus Limited
Author photo by Joanne Mikkelsen
Text design by Tannice Goddard, Soul Oasis Networking
Printed and bound in Canada by Friesens for Johnson Gorman Publishers

Acknowledgments
Financial support provided by the Alberta Foundation for the Arts, a beneficiary of the Lottery Fund of the Government of Alberta.

COMMITTED TO THE DEVELOPMENT OF CULTURE AND THE ARTS

National Library of Canada Cataloguing in Publication Data
Mikkelsen, Glen
Checkered courage
Includes bibliographical references.
ISBN 0-921835-62-0
1. Glass family. 2. Glass, Iris. 3. Chuckwagon racing—Alberta. 4. Rodeo performers—Canada—Biography. 5. Stunt performers—Canada—Biography. I. Title.
GV1833.5.M537 2002 791.8'4'0922 C2002-910248-0

5 4 3 2 1

Contents

Acknowledgements

The Glass family built this book. Thank you to Reg, Tom, Tara, and Jason Glass, Babe Lauder, and the rest of the family for so intimately revealing their stories. And particularly, thank you to Iris Glass for so wholeheartedly supporting this project. The Glass family has earned its stall in the barn of western Canadian legends.

Thank you also to the Calgary Exhibition and Stampede, editors Sue Sumeraj and Gillian Watts, and photographers Paul and Carol Easton for weaving this book together. My family, my friends, and chiefly my wife, Joanne, kept this writer's pen twitching.

This book is dedicated to the late Dr. Grant MacEwan for his great passion for western people, and particularly to my recently deceased father-in-law, Bob Hatfield, my grandfather, Chris Mikkelsen, and my mother, Louise Mikkelsen. Their wisdom and laughter are missed.

Last but not least, during the solitary days I spent writing, our dog was a dependable buddy. Looking like a Jim Henson Muppet, and running like a swamp rat from *The Princess Bride*, Begbie keeps the fun flowing in our home. As one neighbor blurted, "Geez, that's a funny dog." Thanks, Begbie.

A High River, Alberta, gravestone reads:

Bill Pender
Old Time Cowboy
Died 1936

When the final summons comes
From the court house in the skies
And the judge of all the judges
May he deem it no surprise
If I ask him but one favour
He may give it no one knows
Send me back to fair Alberta
Where the Highwood River flows

For Joanne

Introduction

Life in Black and White

The range shimmered beyond Armandine's vibrating hood; the gravel road crunched beneath her tires. Iris and Ron Glass drove north towards Coronation, Alberta, with the truck's windows rolled wide open. The three-ton Ford was loaded high with a dismantled chuckwagon, harnesses, and some fidgety horses. The miles ticked by. Magpies and coyotes scattered, watching them pass. It was hot. It was dusty. And they were broke.

The year was 1946. Ron and Iris had just left a chuckwagon show in Hanna, Alberta. A few hours before, when they were loading Armandine (named for her previous owner, still stencilled on her doors), a spunky wheel horse had kicked in their chuckwagon's front panel. Travelling on oats and hopes, Ron and Iris had little money left to continue their wagon racing, let alone spare cash to replace the missing board.

Braking at a lonely T-intersection, Ron noticed a fallen checkerboard sign, the type used to warn drivers that the road is coming to a deadend. The black-and-white sign lay neglected in the prairie grass, and it looked ideal to replace the broken panel on the chuckwagon. Ron stopped, jumped out, and threw the sign into the truck. After they arrived in Coronation, Ron cut and attached the sign to the wagon. It was a perfect fit. Twenty-one-year-old Iris was so impressed by the distinctive black-and-white pattern that she found some paint and covered the rest of their red wagon with the same squared design. The checkerboard chuckwagon was born.

Almost immediately, checkers became the Glass family's signature — their trademark. Soon, they appeared on the driver's and outriders' shirts, on the outriding horses' saddle blankets, and even on the water buckets. Today at the Glass farm, the black-and-white squares appear on a birdhouse, a treasured roll of toilet paper, and a crocheted crucifix hanging in the living room. Even Checkers, the cat, is colored black and white.

Checkers are the coat of arms of a daring and fascinating western Canadian family. The Glass story tracks the settlement of the West and the tradition of professional chuckwagon racing. The family's dreams have always been grain-fuelled, horse-harnessed, and swirled in spraying dust. Their ballad sings of flying manes and pounding hooves. And their black-and-white squares add to the richness of the western mosaic that tiles southern Alberta.

To appreciate the Glass family, you need to understand where they live. The family farm is located east of High River, Alberta, fifty kilometers south of Calgary. High River is the centre of Alberta's ranching country. Hutterites, the original black-hatted cowboys, mingle with the rest of the community. The town's businesses include Bradley's Western Wear and Saddlery (established 1900), the Moovie Ranch video store, and a Cargill Foods plant. The Cargill plant can process 3,600 head of cattle per day, smoldering the agricultural incense of burning cattle hair.

High River is proud of its western roots. Murals painted on the sides of buildings illustrate cattle drives, buffalo jumps, and its famous hometown sons, writer W.O. Mitchell and former Prime Minister Joe Clark. Located across from the museum is Paul Van Ginkel's 1993 mural, *Chuckwagon Races*. It depicts local teamsters Ron Glass, Lloyd Nelson, Hank Willard, and Tom Glass charging their outfits straight at the viewer and seemingly into a parking lot.

Encircling High River are spacious foothills and plains. To the west, the foothills roll into "The Rocks" — the Rocky Mountains. Their grey silhouettes cut a jagged edge into the horizon. To the east, the prairie stretches uninterrupted towards Saskatchewan. Here, humanity seems small. Fence posts and barbed wire twang into the vast expanse. Aluminum feed bins are echoing drums in the summer hailstorms. The few trees have been cultivated to protect homes and property from the roar of the Chinook.

In southern Alberta, the Chinook's western winds whistle habitually over the foothills and plains. The Chinook's arrival is announced by a distinctive arch stretching from north to south in the "big sky." Below, at fescue level, the potent winds soon begin to howl, clearing the country of snow and moisture. This visible power has nurtured many fables. One yarn tells of a teamster driving his horses from Longview to High River. It was winter, and the snow lay thick and heavy on the ground. He harnessed the team, hitched them to the sleigh, and set out. Halfway to High River, he heard a whistling noise. The cowboy knew what it was — a Chinook stealing up on him. He threw the lines to his horses and, driving like blazes, managed to keep ahead of the warm wind. With sweat foaming on their chests, the horses charged into town and towards the livery barn. The teamster stabled his team and headed to the nearest saloon for a much-needed shot of tongue oil. "Boys!" he bellowed, "'T'was all I could do to keep the front runners on the snow. Those back runners was raisin' a hell of a dust storm!"

This territory of Chinooks, ranches, and cowboy characters was also the home of Guy Weadick. Born in New York, Weadick organized and promoted the first Calgary Stampede in 1912. Throughout his life, he shared the romance and the hospitality of the West. In 1920, Weadick and his wife, Florence LaDue, built their Stampede Ranch west of High River. Every June, High River remembers their "loyal son of his adopted West" by hosting the Guy Weadick Memorial Rodeo.

In 1923, in conjunction with the Calgary Stampede, Weadick developed the first professional chuckwagon races. They reflected the wild, rowdy, and furious contests in which camp cooks vied to see who could strike camp and dash first to the local barn or saloon. Weadick enticed cowboys from the local ranches to compete. The fundamentals of chuckwagon racing have changed little since then.

Modern chuckwagon races consist of three to four "outfits." Each outfit includes one chuckwagon, one driver, and four horses to pull the wagon. The two horses hooked up in front are the "leaders," and the two horses closest to the wagon are the "wheelers." Joining the driver are two or four mounted outriders. In a four-outrider race, each man has a job based on the original open-range races. One outrider steadies the lead horses before the horn blows. Meanwhile, the other three stand at the rear of the wagon. When the klaxon sounds, one outrider throws a "stove" into the wagon (now a ten-pound plastic tub), and the other two each throw a tent peg into the wagon box. In races using only two outriders, there are no tent peg men. At the start of the race, the wagons and outriders perform a figure-eight pattern around two barrels. They then circle a five-eighth-mile oval track to a wire finish. Time penalties are assessed for infractions and added to the outfit's "running time" (the time taken to complete the barrel turns and circle the track). The outfit with the lowest total time is declared the winner.

From May to mid-August, chuckwagon races thunder all across western Canada. In mid-July, the wagons roar into Calgary. As in Weadick's era, the Stampede's Rangeland Derby is the show every cowboy strives to win. The ten-day competition is the most grinding, the most publicized, and the most respected. The Calgary Stampede defines champions.

On racetracks across North America, the Glass family are proven winners. They have won eight World championships and eleven Calgary Stampede championships. The Glasses have "seen the elephant" — four generations of drivers have experienced unrivaled adventure and glory. Four generations have raced, grieved, and triumphed around the wagon track. They have gloried in all the emotions and drama that western life can offer.

The Glasses' larger-than-life enterprises inspire tall tales. This is a family that arrived in the world with leather lines in their hands, cowhide boots on their feet, and buckles at their waists. Stallions were their pets and badgers their playmates. When chilled and lonesome, they would cuddle in a den of rattlesnakes. For breakfast, the Glasses eat toasted dynamite topped with spiked cactus. Their tonic is arsenic and alkali. Mosquitoes break beaks on their skin, and wolves howl along with their songs. They will harness anything with hair on it, and have driven a few critters too tough to grow any hair. She-grizzlies, bull moose, and sizzling bolts of lightning pull their wagons. And when they want a race, they challenge prairie twisters.

To find the cradle of these stories, look for the checkerboard mailbox. Turning east off Alberta's Highway Two, you find the Glass farm between the Hirsche Hereford Palace and the Mazeppa Gas Plant. Here the earthy smell of cattle manure, the faint odor of sour gas, and the crisp foothills air mingle to create a scent that is distinctly Albertan.

Dominating the Glass farm is the cherry-red horse barn, built in 1912. It rightfully looms above the property, given the family's devotion to horses. The barn is a functional equine shrine. In here, the family's sense of purpose and their passions have been sheltered, cared for, and loved.

Along with the stables, corrals, and a quarter-mile line of caragana bushes, three houses sit on the Glass farm. Reg, Jason, and Iris Glass each own a home — they jokingly refer to the farm as their own Hutterite colony. Iris lives in the homestead's original farmhouse, built in 1910. Appropriately, there are three hitching posts in front of the house. But, Iris laughs, "The hitching posts are just for show. I told them not to, but the boys hitched up a team of wagon horses to the posts. Sure enough, the horses raised their heads and pulled the posts out."

Through her stories, Iris Glass will take us into her family's barn. She and her children, Reg, Tom, and Tara, her grandson Jason, and her sister Babe will welcome us into their motorhomes. With them we will go down the road and behind the applause. The Glasses will reveal to us their lives and passions — the furious pursuit of chuckwagon racing, the breathtaking speed of horse racing, and the celluloid illusions of motion picture stunt and film work. Let's meet our guides:

The hub of the family's wagon wheel is Iris Glass. Iris was constructed from the landscape around her — from the bold prairie earth and the boundless Alberta sky. She radiates the freedom of the land and the beauty of its distinctive majesty. The unending skies mirror her optimism and zest for living. Her weathered hands, rugged and strong, reflect a resourceful femininity. Iris's strength is rooted in the soil, in the foothills, in the West.

Born in 1924, Iris has spent her life on the chuckwagon circuit. A pioneer and a role model, she is considered chuckwagon racing's matriarch. She remains one of the most respected people associated with the Calgary Stampede. To thousands, she and her family's name are symbolic with the Greatest Outdoor Show on Earth. But although she has been labeled "Queen of the Chucks," the burly wagon cowboys call Iris simply "Gram." Iris says, "I must be 'grandma' to fifty-nine kids, and they always ask me about their horses. I love it." She mentors new cowboys, giving them the support of her years of experience. Offering tips, advice, and even a bed to sleep in, she nurtures the sport she loves both on and off the track.

Tough, spirited, and engaging, Iris is a poker-playing grandmother who'll call your bluff any day. "Bucking the tiger," she has turned a lifetime of gambles into triumphs. Her son Tom states, "We're a very competitive family, which probably comes from my mother. Mom is the driving force." Through Iris, the Glass family sustains their ambition to succeed.

Iris's eldest son, Reg, was born in 1946. Tall, lean, and with the cool composure of Lucky Luke, Reg never felt compelled to drive a chuckwagon professionally, but he did win five outriding buckles in Calgary. A natural horseman, Reg turned his skills to training racetrack thoroughbreds. With his unusual combination of wagon racing and racetrack experience, Reg succeeded like no other trainer. Married to Jeanne (Christian), Reg has two children, Ronnie and Reva.

Cast in the mould of Buffalo Bill Cody or John Wayne, Iris's son Tom is an impressive western celebrity. With handsome cowboy features and eyes sparkling with youthfulness, he looks every inch a silver-screen movie star. He is, in fact, literally a Calgary Stampede poster boy. In 1998, to celebrate the seventy-fifth anniversary of chuckwagon racing, Tom's portrait was prominent on the Stampede's poster. Portraying him driving his chuckwagon right at the viewer, the poster ably captures the man's magnetism.

Born in 1948 and named after his grandfather, Tom Lauder, Tom raced chuckwagons for the thrill of winning. And win he did. When Tom retired from racing in 1999, he had driven to four Calgary Stampede Rangeland Derby championships, three World championships, two Cheyenne Frontier Days victories, and more than twenty-five career victories. With his first wife, Bonnie James, Tom had a daughter, Corry, and a son, Jason. He married his second wife, Joanne (Collard), in 1982, and they have one daughter, Kristy.

Iris's only daughter, Tara, was born in 1950. Named after the county in Ireland from which her great-grandfather John Lauder emigrated, Tara is graceful, poised, and assured. She, too, followed the lure of horses and wagon men. Married first to outrider and driver Eddie Wiesner, she had one daughter, Kim. In her second marriage, to driver Richard Cosgrave, she had two sons, Colton and Chad. Tara is a courageous woman who has bravely celebrated a life of challenge and change.

Babe Lauder, Iris's sister, was born in 1932. Her heart also beats to the cadence of horses' hooves. A true horsewoman, Babe competed in every horse event she could enter and jockeyed thoroughbreds until her late thirties. Now living in Maple Ridge, B.C., Babe continues to train horses and works as a wrangler in the British Columbia film industry.

Jason Glass is chiselled from the same granite as his grandfather, Ron, and his father, Tom. Born in 1970, Jason was fated for chuckwagon prominence. At age sixteen, during his rookie year of outriding, Jason won the Calgary Stampede, and he won again outriding for his dad in 1994. Shifting his attention to driving, he won his first World championship in 2000. Jason is depicted, along with his father and the Glass's checkered chuckwagon, in a full-scale diorama in the Round-Up Centre at Calgary's Stampede Park. Jason seethes with the resolute energy of a confident, strapping, robust man, and he is carrying the Glass name into the twenty-first century.

In their colloquial prairie style, the Glass family will demonstrate their strength, humor, and resolution. They will share why they follow a western lifestyle revolving around tradition, no matter how high the cost. They will detail how their lives, like their wagons, have contrasted black and white: sorrow and joy, defeat and victory. Their chuckwagons symbolize an unrivaled family's ambition and pluck, played out on Alberta's plains.

Our journey traces the life and story of Iris Glass, but it is not confined to her alone. As we follow her biography, we will also meet some of her family and hear their stories. The family's voices are shared throughout this book, yet by no means is this a comprehensive history of the Lauder/Glass/Cosgrave clan. The stories here reveal some of the family's public successes, as well as their private anguish. They come from around the kitchen table, the tack room, and the motorhomes. They present the web of emotions woven in their memories and their hearts. The Glass story is not just about what they have done; it is also who they are.

At the beginning of the twenty-first century, the Glass family epitomizes western Canadians' grit. The romantic West is not dead. Cattle country remains a land of picturesque and stirring events. Passion and challenge continue to flourish beyond the stuccoed repetition of Calgary's subdivisions. The dreams of long ago continue to resound and renew themselves with a new millennium kick.

Western Canada is still an old land filled with new people. Its inhabitants are compellingly legendary, dramatic, and engaging. The measure of people in ranching country continues to have little to do with stampedes and barroom brawls, and everything with how the tempestuous landscape forges human character. The Canadian West continues to breed individuals and legends that match the grandeur of its mountains and its endless plains. Many of the West's legends are derived from the nineteenth century: immigration, confrontations between whites and Natives, and the boom-and-bust cattle industry. But the twentieth century is now responsible for more than half of the West's popular tales, producing equally compelling issues and characters: booms in wheat production, the Depression, oil and gas discoveries, and migrations to the West and back again. The movers of the country are still people rich in desire, opportunity, and disappointment. Stories of tragedy, hope, and risk-taking persist, with distinctive twists.

Iris Glass and her relatives are a link to the West's greatest stories. Their careers and their lives are quintessentially western. Over the last 120 years, they have taken part in the settlement, development, and celebration of the West. Arriving on the Plains with the Mounted Police, staking pioneer homesteads, glorying in chuckwagon championships, or perpetuating an idealized West in Hollywood movies, the Glass family has ridden into the folklore of the West.

And now, like the reversed black and white of a film negative, the Glasses have become the myth. Their lives are the foundation of a western movie — they produce the horse opera. Their script reveals determination and success amid contention and sadness. Every frame encapsulates emotions, memories, and aspirations. The reels are a constant litany of life and death, vitality and spirit.

But with the Glasses' motion picture, there is no ending and no beginning. There is only life, and all that it offers a remarkable family. Here they generously expose scenes from that life. The room darkens . . . the images flicker . . . horses are heard nickering to the west.

The Glass story begins.

1

Carrying On

Rod would want us to carry on the sport he loved.
He wouldn't want it any different.
— IRIS GLASS

Iris Glass pulled herself up the last few rungs of the ladder to the Calgary Stampede's media booth — the "Eye in the Sky." It was Wednesday, July 14, 1971. Iris joined fellow CFAC radio announcer Lorne Ball, and together they prepared to broadcast live the forty-eighth running of the Stampede's Rangeland Derby. Below their booth, the rumble of the crowd filled the shaded seats. Iris recalls, "We were up in the old grandstand. We were right at the very tip-top of that old thing. It was just small up top there. You used to have to climb a ladder going straight up."

Across from the crowd, behind the racetrack, the cowboys were engrossed in hooking their horses to the wagons. As usual, tension and anxiety filled the barns, the cowboys and horses both tautly anticipating the evening's competition. Among these cowboys, Iris's husband, Ron, and her sons Reg, Tom, and Rod, were joining their teams and saddling the outriding horses. Ron would be driving two wagons during the evening's races, Tom was driving one wagon, and both Reg and Rod were outriding. All three sons would be outriding behind their dad's chuckwagon for two heats.

Of the three brothers, Rod was the youngest. At eighteen, he was already an accomplished jockey and outrider. Cheerful, friendly Rod knew how to ride horses and how to win. He had already won the Southern Alberta Turf Club's trophy for the most points as a jockey on the bush circuit.

Iris watched for her sons to come onto the track. For fifteen years she provided color commentary on the radio. "Ronnie didn't think it was a very good idea, because I wasn't *there* all the time to help hitch and unhitch. I did it anyway, but as soon as it was over I was back to the barn."

The evening's first two wagon heats were swift and smooth. For the third heat, Ron Glass brought his outfit sponsored by A.A. Bishop onto the track, his sons and their horses joining him at the barrels. At the klaxon's roar, Ron and his outfit deftly turned the barrels. Reg, Tom, and Rod leapt on their horses and surged forward amid the dust, joining Ron in fast pursuit.

As the four wagons, thirty-two horses, and twenty men turned the first corner, a chuckwagon clipped Rod's horse, knocking it down. Rod and the horse each got to their feet, ready to rejoin the race. But as Rod tried to jump back into the saddle, another outrider and his horse collided with them. Both horses fell, landing on top of Rod and crushing him. A portable stage hid the first turn from the spectators' view, and most onlookers did not see what happened.

When she was broadcasting and a wreck occurred, Iris says, "You didn't really say anything on the radio. We said, 'We have to stop the races for a few minutes, because there's a horse in trouble' or 'There's a wagon in trouble.' That's about all you said."

When he had finished the race, Reg headed over to where his brother lay on the track. "I was one of the first ones to Rod. I knew the doctors in Calgary who volunteered for the wagon races. I came around, pulled up by Rod, and I jumped off my horse. There was a lot of blood hanging out. I said, 'How does he look? How does he look?'

"The doctor said, 'I think he's got a broken nose, and that's where all the blood came from.'

"'Ah, shit. Thank God,' I said. I went away on my horse and never thought any more about it. I asked our friend Sandy Shields to go to the hospital with Rod, to see what was going on."

Ron Glass went on to drive his second outfit, sponsored by Dan Johnson. Tom drove his own outfit and also outrode with Reg. Tom recalls, "It was a positive-thinking thing. You just think, 'He'll be fine. He's hurt, but he'll be all right.' We rode in three or four more heats."

After the night's final race, Reg rode past Sandy Shields, who had returned from Holy Cross Hospital. "Sandy was standing along the side as we were riding out, and he said, 'Rod didn't make it.'" Eighteen-year-old Rod Glass had died from irreparable internal injuries.

Reg remembers, "I didn't believe it. You just totally deny it. I rode up to Dad and said, 'Sandy said Rod didn't make it.' Dad said, 'Oh bullshit.' Same thing — he just refused to believe it."

Iris says, "All of our kids had fallen off horses, but not tragic like that. You never thought the worst. We just knew he'd fallen off a horse and they'd taken him to the hospital." Memories of the hospital stayed with Iris for years. After that evening, she states, "I couldn't go to the Holy Cross Hospital. Oh, I couldn't do it. Two or three of my friends were patients in there, and they even took Ronnie in there one time, but I said, 'I'm not going there. I can't go.' I never went in it again. Never."

Reg affectionately remembers his brother. "You had to know Rod. Tom and I, and a lot of our relatives, are all pretty aggressive people. We look after ourselves — kind of rough, tough stuff. But Rod was just the sweetest kid in town. He didn't have any aggression in him at all — just a big smile all the time."

The sport, the lifestyle of chuckwagon racing, which had given so much to the Glass family, had abruptly taken too much away. Tom says, "I can remember sitting in the barn and cussing the chuckwagons — hating them. I was just mad. I had to be mad at something, so I was mad at them. You think about quitting, and you think about being pissed off. And the next day, the sun comes up — there it is and it's all going on. They were going to hook again. I guess me sitting on my ass in the barn wasn't going to make any difference. Everybody else was going out there."

The next night, after one minute of silence from the grandstand, Ron, Tom, and Reg returned to race, and Iris went back to the broadcast booth. Two days later, the family and the chuckwagon community congregated in High River for Rod's funeral. The pallbearers were the greatest wagon drivers of their generation, including Ralph Vigen, Bill Greenwood, Tom Dorchester, Hally Walgenbach, Lloyd Nelson, and Bob Cosgrave. That evening, after the funeral, the cowboys and their families congregated to race at the Calgary Stampede. For the Glass family, it was a fitting tribute to Rod's passions, a veneration of his memory and the family's horse-centered fellowship.

"Mom and Dad were so strong through it," Tom recalls. "I know how much my mom was hurting, but she was still there. She didn't go away and hide. Same with Dad — he probably never said two words for a week, but he was always there."

"Rod would've wanted us to go on, carry right on," says Iris. "It'd be worse if the cowboys ever had to quit. If there wasn't any more racing for them, it'd just ruin their lives. If they didn't race, their lives would be half stopped. We don't want that to happen — you'd be sad the rest of your life."

She adds, "Rod would have thought it was a horrible, silly thing to quit racing just because of him. And we carry on knowing that he wanted us to."

But she admits, "It wasn't easy. We'll never forget him."

To preserve Rod's memory, the family introduced the annual Rod Glass Memorial Trophy in the year following the accident. It is presented to the most improved outrider of the year, and both Rod's brother Tom and Tom's son, Jason, have won the trophy.

Despite Rod's accident, the Glasses understood that chuckwagon racing continued to be their core passion — their work and their play. The sport defined them; their aspirations were entwined in its wheels. They were born to sit in a plywood box, racing at forty-five miles per hour. As Tom Glass declares, "Chuckwagon racing is part of us, part of what we are." Their commitment to chuckwagon racing and its community is an enduring Glass trait. They persevere. They accept the sport's risks and its rewards. And after four generations, the Glasses continue to be its leaders. They are maintaining a family custom and a way of life that extends to wagon racing's earliest origins.

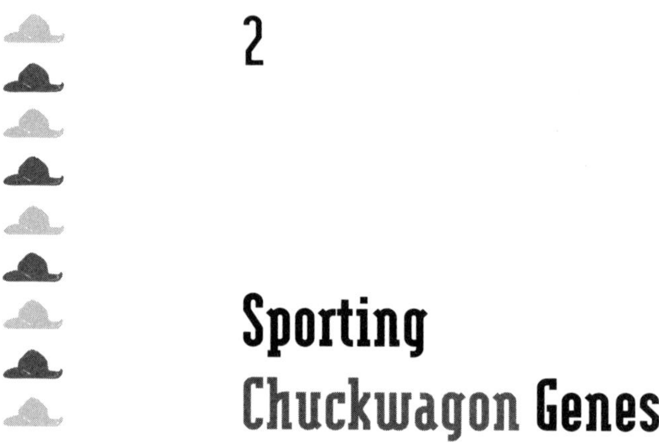

2

Sporting Chuckwagon Genes

I rode every horse I could sneak on.
— IRIS GLASS

Iris Glass has seldom slowed down since she was born on December 1, 1924, in her aunt's home in Innisfail, Alberta. "It happened so fast, I never got to the hospital. I've been in a hurry from the get-go." She was born into a family of pioneers and gifted horse people. Her Irish grandfather, John Drought Lauder, came to western Canada with the North West Mounted Police in 1884. Lauder served with Major Hatton's Alberta Rifles in the 1885 Rebellion, and he worked to maintain the peace between Natives and non-Native settlers.

Lauder's most celebrated police assignment was immortalized by the renowned American artist Charlie Russell. In Russell's painting *Single*

Handed, Lauder is depicted in his red serge uniform, mounted on his horse, and surrounded by tepees and Natives as he arrests a Native warrior. Iris recounts, "An Indian had murdered two women, and he had their scalps hanging on his belt. The police said, 'We've got to get him and bring him in.' Lauder said, 'I'll go get him.'" Lauder knew the accused; riding alone, he brought him back for trial.

Lauder stayed with the NWMP for four years. After leaving the police force, he practiced veterinary medicine. For years, he was known as "Grand Doc." Iris says, "Even though he was a vet, he still fixed people's aches and pains, like broken arms and legs. He even delivered babies." Grand Doc also raised cattle and trained horses. He registered the O Bar O cattle brand and the five-pointed-star horse brand. Both these family brands are still used by Tom Glass.

John married Marguerite Thompson, and together they raised two sons and four daughters. Lauder died in 1934, at the age of eighty-seven, in Innisfail, Alberta. He was buried in his NWMP uniform, complete with pillbox hat.

Tom Lauder, John and Marguerite's second son, was born in Calgary's Elbow Park in 1886. Tom lived and breathed horses, and he grew up to be a gifted cowboy. As one of the original 1912 Calgary Stampede contestants, Tom rode bucking horses and later competed in wild-cow milking. But horses remained his specialty.

Lauder's horse prowess earned the affections of Goldie Zierke. Friend Rita Cole said, "Goldie was the most beautiful woman riding a horse that I think I've ever seen." Originally from Bellingham, Washington, Goldie immigrated with her parents to homestead at Huxley, Alberta, near Tom's farm. There they met, and were married in 1913. In time, Tom and Goldie raised eight children: five boys and three girls. Jack, Bob, Kaye, Iris, Bill, Jim, Babe, and Troy all grew up chasing and riding horses. In Iris's words, "They brought the whole family up to be horse people."

As they had with her grandfather, neighbors called upon Iris's father for his veterinary medicine skills. "At different places we lived, when people had trouble with their animals, they'd call Dad. He was a rancher, but he had learned so much from Grand Doc that he could fix quite a few things, too."

In the 1930s, Alberta was plagued with an epidemic of equine encephalitis ("sleeping sickness"). Horses that contracted the airborne virus would circle in a zombielike state; if they walked into a fence, that is where they stayed. The disease permanently affected a horse's mental health, effectively disabling it. Tom Lauder travelled across Alberta vaccinating horses against sleeping sickness. While he was away, one of the family's favorite ponies became infected. The horse was too treasured to lose. Using a caustic, Lauder made an opening in the horse's skull, into the brain, relieving the pressure on it. Unlike most horses that contracted sleeping sickness, the Lauder pony lived.

When Iris was a young child, she and her family lived on various Alberta ranches, from Morley to Cochrane to Innisfail. With horses constantly around, Iris recalls, "I was a terrible tomboy. I'd rather do anything outside than do anything else. My sister Kaye says, 'Every time we finished eating and it was time to do the dishes, through the window you could see Iris streaking away, and she was gone.'" Iris preferred to be in a musty stall rather than at the disinfected kitchen sink. "I always said I'd rather clean the barn than do dishes. I think I still do. I always had a horse, and I'd run to the barn, get the horse, and away I'd go. I'd hide somewhere till the dishes were done.

"I must've ridden a million miles in my lifetime. My whole life I have loved horses — I was raised with a horse in my hand. Dad always had a Shetland pony, and at age three I learned to ride. I never got hurt really bad, except my Shetland pony dumped me off once and I broke my arm. I was coming down a hill, chasing a cow, and it ran between some trees and off I went. I came home with my arm in a sling, but I was on the same horse the next day."

Iris moved up from her pony, quickly learning to ride stockier, more powerful horses. "Dad was a real horse dealer, and lots of times he'd bring one home and I'd be all excited. Dad would say, 'Now, this one you can't ride. I'm telling you now, you can't ride this one, because it isn't broke.

You've got to wait awhile.'" As soon as her dad left the farm, Iris was in the circular corral breaking and riding the new horse. "I'd put a bridle on them first and lead them around. Dad showed me how to throw a blanket on their back, and I'd let that hang around. Gradually, I'd get a saddle on and lead them some more. I'd get them quiet enough leading with the saddle on. Then I'd have to get a hay bale or a pail to get on the horse."

She laughs. "I got bucked off lots of times. But I think when you're a kid, you're so loose that when you get bucked off it doesn't hurt. We never quit doing it. Dad would come home and say, 'Were you playing with that horse?' I'd say, 'Yeah, Dad, I got him broke. He goes really good.' 'Oh Lordy!' he'd say."

One day, a horse bucked Iris off three consecutive times. "My sister Kaye was with me, and she got mad. She said, 'Just stop, you're going to get really hurt.' So then I got real ornery, and told her, 'No, I won't stop. I'll just ride this thing if I have to stay here all night.' And I eventually did."

From Innisfail, the Lauder family moved to just south of Pine Lake, Alberta. Iris and her siblings rode two and a half miles to school from their new home. "When we went to school, every one of us had to ride bareback, because Dad thought it was the safest thing to do. With a saddle, you might get your foot caught in a stirrup." This bareback experience taught Iris how to ride a horse instinctively. "When you jump on a horse bareback, your body learns how to go with the horse. You get balanced something wonderful. It was the only way to teach a kid how to ride. When the horse's body moves one way, you just naturally move with the horse. You purdy near know which way the horse is going to move, as soon as his body moves."

As a jeans-wearing tomboy during the 1930s, Iris did not meet her teachers' fashion expectations. Girls were supposed to wear skirts at school. "First I'd put a skirt on, but since we rode a horse to school, you wore pants underneath your skirt. You were then supposed to take the pants off at school." She chuckles. "I had a fight with every teacher, since I wouldn't take my jeans or cords off. At home, Kaye would tell Mom, 'Iris wouldn't take her pants off! She wouldn't take her riding pants off! She had a fight with the teacher again!' I never learned to like wearing dresses or skirts, but I do once in a while, now. It's a good thing pants came in for all women, or I'd definitely have been an outcast."

Like thousands of Depression-era prairie families, the Lauders stretched their money resourcefully. Iris remembers, "Money was very, very short." While living at the Lone Star Ranch near Innisfail, the family was nearly self-sufficient. "We had purdy near everything that you'd eat, except flour, sugar, coffee, and tea. Mom always had a great big garden, and we had chickens, geese, ducks, pigs, and we'd butcher our cows or yearling steers. . . . We were just an ordinary family with eight kids." To preserve their produce, the Lauders used an icehouse. "In the winter, we'd go to Pine Lake and get blocks of ice cut out from the lake. We brought the ice home, covered it with straw, and it kept meat good for months."

During the summer, Iris was responsible for finding pasture around Innisfail for the family's milk cow. After walking it through Innisfail, she says, "I picketed the cow out on the edge of town. The kids in town used to be fascinated by me leading this cow around to different places."

The family's every penny was precious. Every toy, except skates, was handmade by Iris's father and brothers. "Even though things didn't cost that much, when we needed a new ten-cent scribbler, we used to have to wait and use the best we could until Mom and Dad had enough money to give us that much to spend."

She adds, "I had some cousins in Calgary who had three daughters and were really well off. They used to send us clothes all the time. We loved to get all of them."

One of Iris's most prized childhood possessions was paint. She recalls, "We thought it was the greatest thing in the world if we ever had a can of paint. We treated it just like gold. We painted everything we could find — a little red sleigh, a little red wagon. Once we painted our toys, we thought they were just the grandest things in the whole world."

In the early 1930s, during the heart of the Depression, the Lauder family was dealt a blazing financial blow. On an early summer day, while Iris and Kaye were in school, the family's Pine Lake home burned to the ground. "Mom was home alone in the garden. She saw the smoke coming out, and my baby sister, Babe, was in the house. Mom ran in and saved Babe. We had no telephone, but there were about forty people there in twenty minutes. There was nothing they could do about it. Dad's wagon trophies and a whole rack full of his hunting guns — all burned. Thankfully, the house was a long way from the barn, so no other buildings were burnt." Like many other house fires of the time, it was believed the Lauder fire started from the kitchen's wood stove. "On the side of the stove there were slats to open for a damper, and the wood box always sat beside the stove. They figured a spark jumped out and lit the wood pile."

Iris recalls, "I'll never forget the Red Cross. We had completely nothing, except for what was on our backs. The Red Cross came with a great big truck, and they unloaded blankets, pillows, clothes, and towels. Us kids thought it was about the greatest Christmas there'd ever been, with all this new stuff." The family moved in with the neighbors until Iris's father could build a new house. Since it was summer, at first they lived in a tent house, with a wooden floor and a canvas roof.

Two years later, another family emergency struck. This time, the Lauders were dependent upon their horses for help. It was winter, and Iris was in the grip of pain from appendicitis. She needed to see a doctor, but the doctor's Innisfail office was twenty-two miles away. Iris recalls, "We had to go by sleigh. To keep our toes warm, Mom kept big rocks in the oven all the time." Goldie wrapped several hot rocks in blankets and set them on the sleigh's floor. "Away we went. Dad always had wonderful horses, really good driving teams like you see in the movies. His teams could gallop for ten miles, and lope all the way to Innisfail."

En route, her father gave Iris some prairie medicine. "Most of the people on the farms had a bottle of brandy. Dad was never, ever without brandy. On the way into town, he gave me a teaspoon. I choked, spit, and cried. It was awful, but it was a real pain thing. Dad kept lots of it, because when a horse got sick, he'd squirt a cupful of brandy down its neck. It was great medication. I remember it being horrible-tasting. But when you had a tummy ache or a really bad cold, Mom would make you a drink a teaspoon of brandy and a little hot water and sugar. It wasn't very good, but it'd make you feel better."

Since the Lauders had no telephone, Tom and Iris travelled hard until they reached the first neighbor who owned a phone. Tom phoned a friend in Innisfail and asked him to meet them on the road into town. They arrived safely in Innisfail, and Iris's appendix was promptly re-moved. Iris ponders, "The 'good old days,' they call it. But I was scared. I remember them saying that if we'd been another hour my appendix would've burst."

Besides transportation, the Lauders also relied upon horses for work and play. "We drove the horses for everything — all our farming — and when we went to town for groceries, we took the horses. It was six to eight miles from Pine Lake to Elnora. We also had a cutter that Mom and Dad took to dances all over the country. They'd take all of us kids, and we'd go to sleep in the cloakroom in the schools."

At those community parties, Iris's father was prone to play practical jokes. "Dad and his best friend were always pulling tricks. They went to a school dance one night, and all the babies were in the cloakroom. They snuck in there and took the clothes — the sweater, toque, bonnet, and shoes — off one baby and put them on another one. They mixed their clothes up and away they went home. The families got home and had the wrong baby! We used to travel up to seven miles to a school dance, and since there were no phones the parents had to go around to each place to see who had their baby."

Tom's practical jokes were not limited to dances. "After harvesting, the men used to haul bundles to the threshing machine. You had to wait a long time for the other wagons to get through, and this one old guy used to sit and wait and fall asleep. So he's sleeping there one day, and Dad and his friend went over and unhitched the tugs from his team. Somebody then yelled at this old guy, 'Come on!' The fellow bolted awake, said, *hyaw* to the horses, and away they went, jerking him right off the wagon."

Tom Lauder was a complete horseman. During his lifetime, tractors began to displace horses, yet Lauder never trusted machines. "Dad never had a tractor, and wouldn't have anything to do with them." Years later, when Tom and Goldie owned a truck, Iris recounts, "I don't remember him ever driving to town. It was either by horses or Mom drove. Mom drove Dad everywhere."

After Stampedes were held in 1912 and 1919, the Calgary organizers decided to host the event annually. In 1923, the tradition of a yearly Calgary Stampede began, and Tom Lauder and his horses were there. In '23, Tom competed in the democrat races, in which teamsters raced two horses and a small democrat buggy from a straight start, around the oval track.

During the competition, Tom witnessed the inaugural "Rumble on the Range" — the chuckwagon races. Captivated by the excitement of wagon racing, he resolved to return with his own outfit. In 1924, five months before his daughter Iris's birth, Lauder won the second annual Calgary Stampede Rangeland Derby.

Tom Lauder's successful initiation into chuckwagon racing was the beginning of the family's neverending pursuit of the sport. Tom again won the Calgary Stampede, in 1927 and 1928, instilling in his children a lasting devotion to the so-called Half Mile of Hell. Iris says, "We kids grew up around wagons. My brother Jack drove a wagon, and Bob, Bill, and Jim were all outriders. Fifteen Lauders have been in the wagon races. Only my brother Troy did not outride; he was too little and his legs were partly crippled. He rode horses, but never got into the cowboy stuff." (Troy died at age twenty-one of kidney disease.)

As a youngster, Iris assisted her father around the wagon barns. "I led the horses around to cool them down, or I'd help hitch up. I had to stand up on the manger to put the collar on the horses, and drag the harness up over the manger to throw it on. It'd take me a good half-hour to get the horse harnessed, but I'd get 'er done."

At that time, rather than using a truck to haul their wagons and horses to the Calgary Stampede, the wagon drivers trailed in by horsepower. Iris recalls, "When I was three or four, there was no such thing as a truck or trailer. Instead, we drove the buggy and chuckwagon. We'd load up and stay in tents. All the other wagon drivers had to do the same. For the six-day Stampede, we set up our tents where the Saddledome now sits. I slept in a tent that Mom brought, and Mom cooked in the tent. The boys had their own tent beside the barn."

It took three days for the Lauder family to travel the dirt roads from Pine Lake to Calgary. Behind their chuckwagon, Tom Lauder trailed ten bucking horses to compete in the Stampede's afternoon rodeo. The horses were not led by halters, but simply walked along, eating grass as they went. All summer, the family trailed their outfit to races and rodeos across southern and central Alberta — Ponoka, Rimbey, Red Deer, Pine Lake, Trochu, and Huxley.

Besides promoting the new sport of wagon racing, in the 1920s Tom Lauder joined a gang of cowboys who were introducing a stampede to Ontario. Tom was an organizer and a competitor, and he shipped a carload of his bucking horses by train. This venture nearly ended his chuckwagon career. Iris says, "Dad was a tough old cowboy. While he was down east, he was riding the bulls, and a bull gored his arm." The bull's horn ripped into Tom's arm, slashing a long, wide cut above his wrist. The Ontario doctors suggested amputating the arm at once; they feared gangrene would set in and threaten Tom's life. "Dad said, 'No, you're not cutting it off. Leave it on, or I'll sew it myself.' So they sewed it up as best they could, and he had a long scar." Tom used his veterinary skills to keep the wound clean from infection. Iris laughs, "Years later, when he was back in the hospital, they tried to find a pulse and the nurse said, 'You have no pulse. You must be dead.' After they fixed Dad, he had no pulse in his left hand."

In 1939, Tom Lauder's wild, sixteen-year wagon-driving career ended abruptly after a serious accident. “Dad tipped his wagon over, coming around the bottom barrel, and broke all the bones in his body. Dad quit, and my brother Jack took over. Dad still helped the kids practice and turn, hitch up, and break horses.”

Following Tom’s wreck, Goldie could no longer bear to watch her son’s barrel turns. She would stay behind a bucking chute, hide her head, and wait till the barrel turns were over before she could watch the rest of the race. Because she was hiding her head, Goldie missed seeing an impatient horse push her son Bob into a wagon. Bob was outriding and throwing stove. When the horn blew, his horse jumped, knocking him into the stove rack. Bob was knocked unconscious and toured the track, benumbed, in the wagon.

Bob’s comical accident was followed by a much more serious one several years later. Iris’s teenaged brother Bill was outriding behind Hally Walgenbach’s wagon. “Bill’s horse fell, he went underneath the wagon, and the wagon ran over his head. He had a hor-rible concussion. He was in Calgary’s General Hospital for almost two years. It was a horrible, sad thing. He was such a cowboy — he could ride anything. Bill didn’t know who he was. We didn’t think he’d ever come through. He had his mattress on the floor, because he’d fall out of bed.

“Bill went home with Mom and Dad, and stayed with them for a long time. He got epilepsy. Epilepsy is the most horrid thing I’ve ever seen in my life. After Mom and Dad were gone, Bill stayed alone in their little house in Elnora. He took a terrible amount of medicine for the epilepsy. Kaye and I would go up and houseclean.” Bill was later moved to the mental health hospital in Ponoka, where he lived for almost two years. Iris adds, “He was okay to visit, but he couldn’t remember different things. He knew Kaye and I, but I think we were the only ones he knew. When he went, it was quite a blessing — he had no life whatsoever. Bill was about sixty years old when he died.”

For wagon cowboys, injuries are part of the contest and the risk. “All the guys have been hurt a little bit,” Iris states simply.

Tom Lauder — King of the Cowboys

Tom Lauder — the famous stampeder —
Drove a chuckwagon to honour and fame
But since he's had a bad smash-up,
Poor Tommy, he's ne'er been the same.

He was Calgary's best driver for years.
He's got the trophy in his name;
He's got four of the best trained horses;
He was always ahead of the game.

He was a famous wild-cow milker.
He was always first to be done;
He'd get to the judges ahead of them all.
Oh boy! I'll bet it was fun.

Now this is the end of my story
Of life on the Alberta plains;
We'll take off our hats to the King of them all,
T.B. Lauder, the King of the range.
(yodel)

"Tom Lauder, King of the Cowboys" was written by Iris's cousin Owen Moore. The lyrics are in Iris's scrapbook, which she started keeping at age ten. The scrapbook is full of melancholy western songs such as "Little Joe the Wrangler," and "There's a Bridle Hanging on the Wall." Iris sang and yodeled these songs to her younger brothers and sisters. She recalls, "God, they'd cry, and Mom would make me quit."

Her sister Babe affirms, "We'd all sit there and bawl."

And Iris laughs, "When I was a kid, I thought I was a really good singer, but I never could sing. I've got the worst voice in the world."

When Tom Lauder retired from wagon racing after his pounding in 1939, he continued training and driving horses on their Innisfail ranch. Although trucks were prevalent by then, he remained committed to grass-fed transportation. The start of World War II re-opened opportunities for teamsters, and Lauder's horses and skills were back in demand. He was needed to assist with one of the most ambitious construction projects ever undertaken in North America. Attracted by the chance of employment and prosperity, Tom and his family wheeled north.

3

A Prairie Gentleman

Ron was a great big, good-looking son of a gun.
— IRIS GLASS

In 1942, Tom Lauder arrived in Dawson Creek, British Columbia — Mile 0 of the Alaska Highway. In response to the perceived military threat from Japan, the highway was rapidly being sliced out of the northern wilderness. Dawson Creek was its construction service point. Tom and his horses arrived first, ahead of the family.

Iris recounts, "Before we moved up there, the hotel across from the Dawson Creek train station blew up and burned to the ground. People were travelling from place to place, and they couldn't find out who half the people were. The hotel's papers and register were all burnt. Dad had his teams cleaning up the mess. There were parts of the people all through the hotel: legs, feet, and heads. Dad found a woman's hand with a beautiful ring on it — just her hand. He took it off, and nobody knew whom it belonged to, so he gave the ring to my mom. Mom wore it a long time. Dad said cleaning it up was the most horrible thing he had to do."

From Innisfail, Iris and her brother Jack freighted twelve more work-horses and Iris's pony. They travelled with the horses for three days on a stock train. Whenever the train stopped, Jack and Iris fed and watered the horses. "Our whole family went up. Dad had fourteen teams of horses working around town. When we moved, there were 250 people, but 1,500 American soldiers arrived, and the town became like a gold-rush boom-town. It just went wild. People lived in the backs of trucks, in sheds, and in tents until they could get something to live in."

The Lauders hauled spring water from the top of Bear Mountain into Dawson Creek. "There was no water in town at all. Dad had six teams going up and down, hauling water all day long, three miles from down-town." Iris and Kaye were responsible for a dray team hauling groceries from the train station to the stores.

In Dawson Creek, Iris Glass was an eighteen-year-old woman surrounded by almost two thousand servicemen — an amorous potpourri. She recalls, "We used to bowl with them, go to shows with them, curled, danced at the army centre, but none ever fizzed on me. They were all friends." One day, Iris's brother Jack said, "Look who I found here!" And in came Ron Glass. Glass was in Dawson Creek driving a gasoline truck, ferrying fuel for highway construction.

A long-time friend of Iris's brothers Jack and Bob, Ron Glass also raced chariots and chuckwagons. Iris had met him through the racetrack, but she had not seen him for several years. He was also nine years older. "I had seen him drive [wagons] at Calgary, but never had much to do with him. When I was ten years old, I thought he was way too old for me. He was an old man! But as I got older, I guess he got younger."

Ron was born in Lethbridge in 1915, to Will and Elizabeth Glass. His father was a renowned grain grower, winning the Farms Crop Trophy for

Champion of Alberta in 1910, 1911, and 1914. Moving to Bowness (now a suburb of Calgary), Will Glass continued to own and train racehorses. In 1930, Will's friend Dad Moore was injured, and fifteen-year-old outrider Ron Glass volunteered to drive Moore's wagon, thus beginning a forty-six–year career. The following year, Ron and his father purchased and organized the first independent Glass outfit to enter the Calgary Stampede.

Ron Glass was a lean, towering man with wide, powerful shoulders. Iris says, "When I first met Ron, he could grab a 45-gallon gas barrel full of gas [weighing 450 pounds] and throw it in the truck. He could lift a chuckwagon box right on the damn wagon. No team ever ran away on him, and God, could he throw hay bales! He never got tired."

In Dawson Creek, Iris remembers, "Ron was a cowboy. He was like my brothers, Jack and Bob, who were the greatest role models to me. I was eighteen years old, and I saw other people had partners, so I figured I might as well have one. I started to go with Ron, and that was it! I could follow the man *and* the sport I love."

In 1944, Tom Lauder sold all his workhorses to farmers in the Dawson Creek area, bought the T. Wyndham Ranch near Elnora, Alberta, and moved the family back south. He returned to buying, breaking, and selling horses and breeding cattle. Tom and Goldie lived at the ranch until they died, Goldie in 1968 and Tom in 1974.

Iris returned to Elnora with her parents. "I was living with Mom and Dad. Ronnie was trucking and living in Calgary. One night he came in with a diamond ring and said, 'This is it. I can't stand being by myself all the time. This is your ring, and we're going to get hitched.'"

Ron said to Iris's father, "I hope you think this is all right, Tom. I'm going to marry this daughter of yours."

"Dad said, 'Oh my God, I hope you can put up with her.'" Iris laughs. "I was an awful tomboy."

After dating for two years, Ron and Iris were now engaged. Several months later, on a cool, early March weekend, Iris and Kaye drove to Calgary to do some shopping and visit Ron. That Friday night, Ron asked, "What'll we do tomorrow?"

Iris said, "Let's get married."

Ron replied, "Okay, that's a good idea. Let's do it."

"So that's what we did," remembers Iris. On Saturday, March 3, 1945, at St. Michael's Anglican Church, Iris and Ron were married in the company of twelve family members and friends. After the wedding, they walked to Ron's truck to drive to a friend's house party. Iris laughs, "I got into the truck with Ronnie, and I slid over. He said, 'All right, we're married now. Now get on your own side.' I said, 'Geeezus!'"

A confident and independent woman, Iris was reluctant to change her surname. "To lose your name, that was just terrible. I was Iris Lauder, and Lauder was just the most fabulous name anybody could ever have. I was so proud of my name, I didn't know if I wanted to change it or not." She wrote a letter to her brother Bob and sister-in-law Eileen, telling them about her wedding, and printed on the envelope, *Iris Lauder Glass*.

Ron said, "Now, you can't do that. You're Iris Glass, and you don't need that Lauder anymore."

Iris grins, "I said, 'To heck with you. I'll just use it if I want.' But I quit using it, and we had a happily married life for thirty-six years." It was a marriage built on humor and discretion. "Ron hated women wearing shorts. I could never wear shorts — Ron couldn't stand it. But back in the early days, women didn't wear shorts out of the yard, past the farm." One time, Ron had broken his ankle wagon racing. "He was gimping around on his ankle really badly. One day, it was really, really hot, so I cut off a pair of jeans. Ron said, 'Now, you're not wearing those shorts.' I said, 'There's nobody here, Ronnie. I can wear shorts. Don't you like looking at my legs?'"

"Aw, no!" he said, "You're not going to wear shorts. And if you don't take them off, I'm going to throw you in the water trough."

"You can't do that," Iris crowed. "You'll hurt your ankle!" But, she recalls, "he just reached around, grabbed me, dragged me all the way to the water trough and put me under. When he got a hold of you, you couldn't do anything. After that he was really, really lame. I said, 'Serves you right. I hope you're really lame.' Every time I got near him, I'd pretend I was going to kick his ankle. He'd jump, and then he'd hurt it again." Still, she concludes, "I didn't wear shorts unless he was gone somewhere. He just didn't like it."

Once they were married, Iris and Ron began creating their own team of outriders. In 1946, their first son, Reg, was born. "I stayed with Ron's mother in Calgary to have Reg. Ronnie was in Cardston up at a wagon race with Billy Collins. One night they unhitched the team, went into the barn, and put all the horses away. Ron said, 'Oh God, Bill, I've got a terrible feeling. I've got to go home right now. Something is wrong with Iris.' He came home and I was having a baby. He had that feeling.

"Pregnancy never bothered me much; it never stopped me doing nothing. I rode horses purdy near to the time that Reg was born." After Reg's birth, Iris adds, "You had to stay in the hospital ten days when you had a baby back then. The day after I got out of the hospital, we went to Trochu and I rode ten races at a gymkhana."

After Reg, Tom was born in 1948, Tara in '50, and Rod in '52. By the time she was twenty-eight, Iris had four children. "Ron always wanted a girl. When Tom was born, the doctor held him and spanked his butt. He said, 'Oh, you've got another lovely boy.'

'Ohh, I wanted a girl.' I was crying, 'cause Ronnie was always giving me such a bad time. But after Tara was born, Ron never quit smiling for three days, because he finally had his girl. And then, finally, Roddy James. I said, 'Now, this is it, Ronnie. This is it.' He said, 'It looks like it should be. We've got quite a crew of hired hands here now.'"

Iris laughs. "I said when we got married we were going to have four outriders to follow the wagon. When Tara was little, she didn't like this at all. She said, 'Mom, what a horrid thing to say, that you didn't want me.' I told her, 'Oh, you were the most wanted kid in the whole world. Your dad wanted every one to be a girl.'"

Through their chuckwagon ventures, Ron and Iris met Johnny Phelan, a prominent central Alberta businessman who owned a string of hotels, ranches, farms, and logging operations. The Phelans and the Glasses developed a lifelong friendship and a sponsorship extending beyond chuckwagon racing.

In the 1940s, unlike today, businesses could not sponsor a wagon and have their names advertised on the wagon canvas. For example, Phelan could not have *The Windsor Hotel in Red Deer* on the wagon tarp. Wagon tarps had to have the name of the driver or the person who owned the wagon outfit. To circumvent the rules, the Glasses and Johnny Phelan claimed the wagon was Johnny Phelan's and that Ron was the driver. Iris says, "Phelan never owned the horses or the wagon, but to get around the early sponsorship rules, it was listed as Phelan's wagon. You couldn't have the hotel name on it, but people all over Alberta knew Johnny Phelan." Phelan sponsored a Glass wagon for ten years.

During the 1940s, there were fewer chuckwagon teamsters, and, unlike today, cowboys could drive more than just one wagon. For example, every evening at the 1947 Stampede, Ron drove three outfits: the Johnny Phelan wagon, the J.S. Armstrong wagon, and the Allan O'Bray wagon. Once, Ron drove five outfits in one night. It was a remarkable feat of physical strength and endurance.

During the winter, Ron worked for Phelan at a logging camp west of Innisfail. As a skidder operator, Ron used draught horses to skid cut logs out from the bush. Iris recalls, "From when Reg was a baby till Tara was born — for four years — we worked at logging camps in the winter. When Reg was about three, he'd drive this horse around, and get a piece of string and tie a little tiny stick to it. Just like his dad, Reg would say *gee* and *haw* [the commands used to turn horses right and left]. One time a fella said, 'Iris, Iris, come look at your kid!' Reg was on this old work-horse, halfway up a sawdust pile, trying to make him go to the top."

After the Glasses had worked in the logging camps, Phelan offered them an opportunity to assist in building two new hotels. "We built Johnny Phelan's hotel in Olds. Then Phelan decided he'd build one in Torrington, east of Olds, so we built that, too, in 1954. When we got it all finished, Johnny Phelan gave the Torrington Hotel to us. His kids were quite damn upset that he gave us that hotel, but we put a lot of work into it." Phelan's gift would ultimately enable the Glasses to buy their High River farm.

While they were running the hotel, the Glasses found their home was popular with local children. Tara recalls, "In Torrington, we had the first television in town. When people came in the bar and left their kids outside, Dad would go to the vehicles, get all the kids, and bring them into our house. Lots of times our living room was full of kids laying on the carpet, watching TV while their parents were in the bar. Dad never let them sit outside."

The Glasses' pony, Skunky, was also a favorite. "In Torrington," Iris recalls, "every kid in the country learned how to ride on Skunky. We'd put a kid on at the hotel's back door — any kid, even if they'd never ridden before. We just sat them in the saddle and said, 'Hang on,' and started Skunky off. He'd go round the hotel, all the way around, back to the back door, and stop."

Reg Glass started school while living in Torrington. One day, Reg's concerned teacher made a private visit to Iris at home. The teacher asked, "Has Reg been sick?" Iris said no.

"Well, he hasn't been to school for two days, Mrs. Glass."

"My heaven's sake," Iris replied, "he hasn't been here." Reg had been leaving home and returning for lunch each day, but the Glasses lived next door to a lumberyard and, Iris laughs, "Turns out Reg had been running through the back fence and crawling underneath a lumber pile. He'd go to sleep, come home for lunch, go back, and go to sleep. For two days he did this. Our dog, Skip, was always out around the lumber pile. I thought, 'There must be something under the lumber pile — a gopher or a rabbit.' Turns out it's Reg!"

Other parent–teacher meetings did not go as smoothly for Iris. A couple of years later, "Reg's teacher called me into the school. She said, 'Reg skipped school. He was misbehaving.' I said, 'He's good in school, isn't he?' She said, 'Yes, very good, but he has his own different ways.'"

Iris seethes. "The teacher added, 'You know what I think it is? It is the life you people lead. The travelling around all summer, and the way he has to live.' I said, 'Lady, you've said a mouthful too much, right there, and you can go to hell. This kid will come back the next day, and you'll teach him through school. And you'll never say that again.' Reg went back to school the next day, and I never heard another word about that kid." She chuckles, "She probably hated me after that, but she never did anything about it — she probably knew she was wrong. They probably talked about me for a week."

Iris and Ron managed the hotel for eight years. Inevitably, Iris says, "It was wonderful when we started, but it got awful tiresome running the hotel. Putting up with people was the worst — putting up with drunks. You pretty well had to drink yourself to keep up with them. They'd get to you after a while." When men picked fights in the hotel, Iris jumped between them. "I'd say, 'All right, you guys, this is it!' They wouldn't dare hit me 'cause Ronnie would kill them, but whenever the women started fighting, I'd have to call Ronnie. O-h-h, the women were wicked when they fought in the bar. I'd get behind the bar and say, 'Sic 'em, girls, sic 'em!' They'd hit you with anything. They'd slap, scratch, and pull your hair."

During the years managing the hotel, Ron ran the bar in the afternoon and Iris oversaw it at night. Iris recalls that, one night, "Some guys came in who Ronnie hadn't seen for a long time, and he started acting smart." She walked over to Ron's table and told him, "Okay, big boy! This is it. You've had your last drink. Now you can leave and go to bed. Not now. Right now." She smiles. "Ron got up and away he went to the house. You should've seen the other men. They just sat there, didn't say one word, and they behaved themselves."

Iris continues, "I could out-holler Ron. I swore at him a little bit, too. When I told him to smarten up, he'd just look and grin. He'd let me know

I was really bossing him, but I wasn't bossing him at all. He'd pretend I was, but I don't think I ever was unless I got really mad. It didn't do me a bit of good."

Although he was a large man, Ron was not a fighter. But he did not hesitate to throw drunks out of the hotel. Iris says, "He had big hands, but I never once saw him shut his fist. If a guy got smart with him, he just slapped him — just knocked him flat on the ground with a slap. He had the best disposition of any big man I saw, and it's a good thing, too, 'cause he was really big."

In the spring of 1960, the Glasses finished with the hospitality business and sold the Torrington Hotel. During that wagon season, Tara says, "We travelled all summer, not knowing where we were going to live." They sought a farm within one hundred miles of Calgary, an area that Ron referred to as "the best place in the world." Ultimately, they bought a farm in High River from Guy Eby. At first, Iris says, "The house was painted yellow, and I hate yellow." In a short time, the house was white with black trim — the family's colors.

The Glasses quickly adapted from town life to farm life. The children had expansive room to explore and play. Iris laughs, "One time, Rod found an old umbrella. The other kids said, 'That's just like a parachute, Rod. Get up there on the ramp, stand up, jump off, and that will be your parachute [the ramp leads to the barn's second floor, and is twelve feet off the ground].' So Rod did. That old umbrella flipped up. He fell and hit the ground, knocking himself cold.

"Nothing in the world could ever beat having little kids. But, oh my God, they keep you on the ball. As they got bigger and got on the horses, they did a lot of falling off and rough stuff, but they never got hurt that bad. If you saw a horse come into the yard with no kid, they'd be out there somewhere."

Generally, the brothers were friends, but Iris recalls once when Tom and Reg's tempers flared. "They were both just a-pounding one another.

Ronnie came strolling out of the barn, walked over, and got each one by the neck. He said, 'Go ahead, boys, fight!' They couldn't reach one another. He just dropped them, and then the fight was over."

After moving to the farm, the Glasses had space for their horses, as well as new animals. Reg says, "After the hotel, Dad thought, 'We're coming to the farm — we're going to be farmers.' We had pigs and chickens and all this goddam stuff." He adds, "A bunch of Dad's friends were auctioneers, and besides the bar, the entertainment was the auction sale. He was always at the sales, buying horses or just bullshitting with the boys. That was a lot of Dad's entertainment." After an auction, Reg laughs, "He'd come home with a great collection of junk every once in a while — wiener pigs, a couple of goats, or sheep. You never knew what the hell was going to get out of the truck once he came back."

Some of Ron's livestock became family pets. Iris recounts, "We had a little miniature goat called History. Every time you opened the door, History was in the house and jumping all over the chesterfield and furniture. We had to keep him out. I had him long enough that he purdy near drove me nuts. So a cowboy got hurt and they had a benefit auction for him. I took History over and he sold for a thousand dollars. Einar Brasso, who bought him, took him home, and they thought he was the cutest little goat. About a month later, he'd given him to some neighbor. Einar said, 'I had enough of History.'"

At another auction, Ron bought a Holstein calf named Ellie. By offering it oats, Rod learned to catch and ride the spotted black-and-white calf. As Ellie grew, she never lost her willingness to let children ride her. Iris says, "As soon as Rod got out of school, he'd go to the pasture and call her: 'Come on, Ellie.' She'd come on the high run. He'd ride her and sometimes she had six kids on her back. God, the kids had fun with her."

But at the Glasses' farm, no animal brought more laughter into their home than Stinky, the snow-white pig. "We raised and sold pigs when we first came to High River. Out of one litter we kept the little runt — we named him Stinky. He was the most beautiful pig you've ever seen, coming from a runt. Rod played with him and played with him. The pig followed Rod everywhere he went. He put ribbons on his neck, fancied him all up, and rode him. Every time you'd leave the door open, Stinky would come into the house." He grew to weigh more than two hundred pounds. Iris continues, "Stinky marched around, boss of the farm. Other kids would come over after school, and they'd try to play a game of hide and seek. Stinky would find every one that hid. He'd take whoever was looking to each kid, grunting all over the yard."

Before the Glasses bought their section, they had looked at numerous farms in the area. Iris remembers, "We looked at a whole bunch of farms around here, and we told friends about the ones that were so terribly dirty and messy. They were awful places. You'd just choke if you'd bought the house.

"One day, my sister Kaye and her husband, Jim, visited, and we were sitting in the kitchen. We didn't have the place long, and I was telling them about all the farms we saw around here — the bad ones, the dirty ones. I'm telling them this story when all of a sudden we hear, 'Hoink, hoink.' Kaye said, 'What in the world is that?' I said, 'Oh my gawd, somebody left the front door open.' Stinky was lying on the rug."

Kaye said, "Talk about dirty houses — we know one now that keeps a pig in the living room." As they roared with laughter, Iris coaxed Stinky outside.

Stinky also sought out higher education. One morning, the pig joined Tara and Rod on their walk to the school bus stop. Iris says, "Stinky got there pretty fast, and when they got in the bus Stinky got in, too. Here he was with all the kids, and they couldn't get him out. He just stayed there — he was going to school. The bus driver had to unload every kid and send them all up our lane before Stinky would get out. After that, Rod and Tara would go around the house the other way to get to the bus. Stinky was always out front waiting for them. They'd crawl through the pasture and Tara would whisper, 'Rod, be quiet, be quiet.'" Stinky would also jump into the family car if a door was left open.

Iris laughs. "The worst time was when I fell asleep sun-tanning on a blanket. I kind of felt this thing on my leg. I jumped up, looking, and Stinky was lying on the blanket with me. He was sun-tanning with me, too — right next to me, stretched right out. I thought if anybody ever came in the yard, they'd have put me away somewhere."

Finally, Ron decided it was time for Stinky to be butchered. "I told him, 'Ron, the kids will never get over this if you do that.' He said, 'We won't tell them. We'll just tell them somebody stole him or he ran away or something like that.' Away he took him. Somehow the kids figured out what happened to Stinky. We had all this pork meat, and the kids wouldn't eat pork for three years. They wouldn't touch it — bacon or anything — because it was Stinky."

On the farm and off, throughout their years together, Ron and Iris were inseparable, a true team. "Even when he was out riding the tractor," Iris reminisces, "I had to go ride with him. We always did everything together." She admits it was an effort to keep pace with Ron — life was a rush. "Ron was one of those guys always in a hurry. He'd come in the house and say, 'I'm going to go do this, are you coming?' 'Well, yes,' I'd say. He'd reply, 'I'm going in about ten minutes.'" Iris would have to get four kids ready and load them into the truck before Ron left.

"Other times, we'd go down the road and stop for a cup of coffee. By the time I got the sugar in mine and stirred, Ronnie would say, 'Let's go.' That's how he ate his meals, too. I'd just be cutting my meat, and he'd say, 'Let's go.' You sure learned to move and eat in a hurry. I still do. I eat awfully fast."

Despite all the miles Ron and Iris journeyed together on prairie highways, they were involved in only one major traffic accident. "We were going to High River," Iris recalls. "It was all stormy and snowing. A snowplough had pulled off to the side of the road, and a gas truck hit the plough. We couldn't see the gas truck and we hit it. My head went up through the windshield, slashing the top of my head, and my arm went through the glove box. Ronnie's head went through the window, and he had all the hair scraped off his head."

Some time before their accident, Iris remembers, a similar gas truck had overturned in the ditch on its way into Calgary. "That driver was caught in it. The truck started to burn, and the guy couldn't get out. He said, 'I'll never get out.' The police came, and he asked them to please shoot him. They couldn't do it, and they had to let him burn."

When Ron and Iris got out of the car after their crash, they saw that the gasoline truck driver's ankle was caught underneath the gas pedal. "We got our car backed out, but they were scared to death the truck was going to burn from all the gas. The driver was just pleading, 'Get me out! Please get me out!' They couldn't get him out, and Ronnie said, 'Let me at him.' Ron took a hold of that bloody gas pedal, just bent the damn thing, and jerked him out. It never did burn. But the driver did come to see Ronnie three or four times later to tell him how thankful he was to get out of there."

Ron and Iris replaced their car and did not feel dissuaded from driving. They knew that next summer the road would call. The racetrack would beckon; it would be time to pack their horses, their tack, and their family. The Glass chuckwagon would be ready to ramble.

Jason Glass roars as his thoroughbreds turn Barrel 3 at the Calgary Stampede, July 8, 1996. *(Paul and Carol Easton, Wagon Photography)*

Tom Glass's checkered outfit cuts around the top barrel at Strathmore (notice the "Glass style" of gripping the lines), August 1, 1997. *(Paul and Carol Easton, Wagon Photography)*

Tom Glass tells his lead horses, Duddy and Faith, to *Go!* as he turns the bottom barrel at Trout Springs, outside of Calgary, June 17, 1995. *(Paul and Carol Easton, Wagon Photography)*

The dust flies as Tom Glass's outfit holds the lead rounding High River's third corner, June 21, 1996. *(Paul and Carol Easton, Wagon Photography)*

Tom Glass guides his outfit to the rail as his late brother-in-law and best friend, Richard Cosgrave, watches closely. Richard drives his celebrated lead team, Duddy and Faith. *(Paul and Carol Easton, Wagon Photography)*

Proudly sporting the canvas of long-time sponsor Shaw GMC, Jason's checkerboard wagon hurtles out of the infield. *(Paul and Carol Easton, Wagon Photography)*

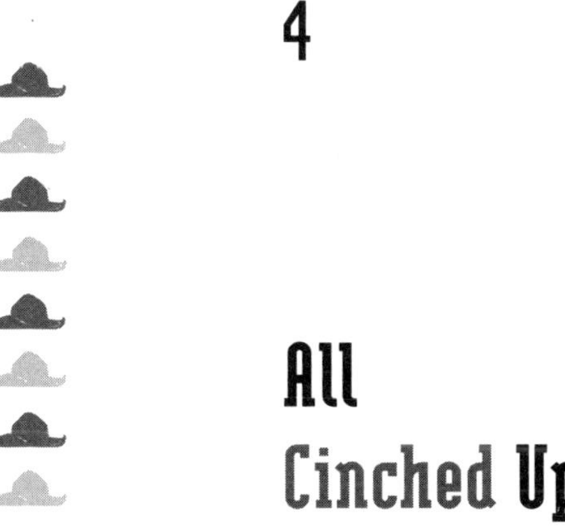

4

All Cinched Up

There was little danger of the horses running off, because Dad was so big and had so much experience. He had so much confidence that he could always handle the horses. It's all touch and experience, and he had that by leaps and bounds. To be bright and strong was a hell of a combination.
— REG GLASS

The pursuit of wagon racing animated Ron and Iris's lives. Recalling their early adventures, Iris says, "When Ron and I first began racing, we'd sleep in a tent. Or we cleaned out the back of the truck where the horses were, rinsed it out with water, and set a tent over top the truck's hoops. We'd sleep in there. If we just stayed for two days, we'd sleep in the back of the chuckwagon. We had sleeping bags and blow-up mattresses. We never had a hotel room or a trailer for years and years. Some families cleaned out a stall in the barn and put clean straw down to stay in there. You tell people that now, and they think you're crazy. I never remember having trouble with the old ways or thinking it was tough."

At the shows, Iris and Ron jointly worked and competed. Between feeding and grooming horses, Iris raced in the afternoon timed events, barrel racing and steer undecorating. Iris explains how to undecorate a steer: "There was a ribbon on the steer's back. You came out of the chute, leaned over the steer, and ripped it off." Iris also drove teams in the two-horse chariot races, rode in flat races, and stood in Roman races.

To spectators, the standing Roman ride seems perhaps the most dangerous race. Two horses are tied together at their cinches and their heads, so they cannot split apart. As the horses gallop a half-mile, the "rider" stands balanced with one foot on the padded back of each horse. Iris states, "Guts is the trick to Roman ride. You start off sitting on one horse, trot along, jump up, and put your foot on each horse. Away you go. You've got pretty good balance with your lines. When the race ends, you just slide down on to one. I can't remember it being hard. It was just fun. It was something more exciting to do than just sit. I never fell off in a race."

In the late 1940s, Ron, Iris, and their young children joined Manitoban Cliff Claggett's touring western show and travelled to eastern Canada. Wagon races, Roman riding, gymkhana events, and pony chariots were all featured entertainment. During one Claggett production, Iris outrode behind a chuckwagon. "An outrider got hurt, and I said, 'I can do that.' Ron told me, 'You just do it at this show, and then you're not doing that anymore.' I said, 'Who are you to tell me what I'm going to do?'" But, she suggests, "I guess it worked — I only raced twice. It's terribly dangerous. Not many girls can jump on like the men can."

Likewise, Iris rarely drove a chuckwagon. She drove four up at home, but only during training. "I used to drive out in the field. Ronnie let me drive, but I couldn't stop the horses. Lots of men can't, either; they need somebody in the wagon to help them when they start training." Iris argues that women are simply not physically strong enough to manage four thoroughbreds. She never drove in a race. Nevertheless, she was photographed driving a wagon in the Calgary barns, creating an enduring fable that she did compete. "A newspaper wanted a picture of me driving, and Ron wouldn't help. I said, 'All right, big boy, you just watch when you go to hitch up tonight. You just watch to see who is going to help you!" Iris hooked up the horses and drove the checkered wagon around the barns. The photo was taken, and she testily returned the horses to their stalls. But, she laughs, "That night, I was probably the first one to Ron's wagon."

Although Iris did not drive chuckwagons, she excelled at the two-horse chariots. Unlike those of the ancient Egyptians or Romans, prairie chariots were constructed from an old automobile axle and two wheels, many of them with wooden spokes. A long pole extended from the two horses past the back of the axle. Padding was fastened to the rear of the pole to make a seat for the charioteer, whose feet rested on the axle. On the tiny pony chariots, smaller, rubber-tired wheels were used, and the basket or carriage was often constructed from a cutaway steel barrel.

In chariot racing, Iris says, "We'd start from the top barrel and only have to turn the bottom barrel — half of a figure eight. We had fast little ponies, and they were just dynamite." She laughs. "One year I was leading the pony chariot–racing standings, and they had the finals at Cranbrook. The last night, I tipped over coming off the bottom barrel. I forgot to lean far enough out the other side. I was going awfully fast, and — *shweet* — out I went. What an awful thing to do the last night, when you're doing so well. I quit the chariots then."

During the 1940s and 1950s, chuckwagon races meant a weekend camping trip, including lunches and goodies for the kids. The races were fun. They were a hobby, not a means of making a living. Iris recalls, "Lots of little Alberta towns had chuckwagon shows. There'd usually be about twelve wagons — four heats with three wagons each — and maybe sixteen wagons competing at Calgary. You didn't need so many horses in those days, since we didn't use outriders [except at Calgary]."

During the 1940s, the cowboys used steel gasoline barrels to mark the barrel turns. If a driver hit one, it generally resulted in a wreck. "Oh gosh, a wagon pretty near tipped over every night. But Ronnie said, 'That's the kind [of barrels] you need to learn how to drive.' You could pretty near count on your hand how many barrels that man hit."

Ron Glass was also proficient with a whip. Until 1948, whips were allowed in wagon races. Even when he was coming off the barrels, Ron held the whip in one hand and all four lines in the other. "He could snap out and hit the lead horse's bum, just like that. Every time. Smooth as can be. He'd just touch them. Whenever Ronnie got off the wagon seat, Reg was on it, practicing driving wagons. One time we were down east, I looked up and Reg had the whip out. He had two little kids tied by binder twine to the wagon pole. Reg was just a-driving 'em, hollering, and he was trying to use the whip, but it was too long for him. I said to Ron, 'For God's sake, hide the whip!'"

Before he raced, Ron always had to check the wagon box for secret passengers. "When the kids were little, we used to hitch up, and you had to look in the back of the wagon, 'cause Reg would be laying down on the floor. He'd crawl in the back and want to go with his dad. He was quiet as a mouse. I often wondered how he could stay quiet for so long." Sneaking a fast wagon ride is a rite of passage among Glass children. When Iris was growing up, she stole a few spins with her father, startling him when she tapped him on the back. Years later, when Tom drove, he, too, had to check for silent hitchhikers, including his son, Jason, and daughter, Corry.

Ron Glass won the Calgary Stampede four times — first in 1941, for his sponsor Lunseth & Higgins, and again in 1946, 1947, and 1949, for Johnny Phelan. Glass continued to win, taking the World championship four times — for Johnny Phelan in 1950, '51, and '52, and for Fiesta Farms in 1965. He also won the Cheyenne Frontier Days championship in 1956, 1966, and 1970. In addition to his wagon-racing triumphs, Ron earned six Canadian wild horse racing titles as a member of Cliff Vandergrift's team. Iris explains: "Ron was the shank man. No horse could get away from him. He just grabbed ahold of the shank, pulled back, and that was it — the horse stayed there. He was a whale of a shank man."

When Ron won three World chuckwagon championships from 1950 to 1952, his lead horses were Casey and Gay-Lady. "They were about the greatest lead team we ever owned. We won hundreds of races in the small towns. For five years nobody outran Ronnie. He just had 'er all cinched — he just knew. That's the only team he never sold."

Throughout his career, Ron Glass was a horse dealer, trainer, trader, and salesman. Iris laments, "Ron was forever starting new teams. He drove me crazy. We'd get a team really working, winning races. Then another driver would want to buy them, and he'd sell them. Ron said, 'You only get offered a good price for a team once, and nobody's going to do it again. I'll just sell them, because I can make another one. There are a lot more horses out there.' I'd get mad. O-h-h, God, I'd get mad."

Iris and the family never adjusted to Ron's constant selling of their best horses. Tom says, "Dad would get a good wagon outfit and then just sell them. He drove us all crazy. He'd be second in Calgary with some horses he'd just started; he'd run real tough. We'd think, 'Boy, next year he's going to kick 'em.' And then he'd sell them all and start with new ones again. Of course, as a kid you want to see your dad win all the time, and all he wanted to do was feed the family. Mom used to talk for all of us. She'd tell him it was pretty disappointing. But he'd show her the cheque [from selling the horses] and say, 'I already won Calgary.'"

Tom adds, "He could've won a lot more races than he did, but he was a horse trader — a dealer. He enjoyed the training and the dealing more than the winning. Dad was a real businessman about wagon racing. That's how he fed the family, and that's how he looked after us. He sold lots of horses, and always had a racehorse that could make some extra money." For Ron, horses were a proud way to earn an income. Iris says, "Ron always said horse manure smelled like money. When the wind blew from the west past the auction market — oh boy, it'd get strong! And Ron'd say, 'It smells like money.' It never bothered him a bit."

In one horse sale, Ron sold a team to Bob Cosgrave, but Bob couldn't drive them, so Ron bought them back. "Everybody used to talk about how Glass could drive strange horses. Ronnie was the greatest at buying a new horse and doing well with it right away. He could drive horses that other guys just couldn't drive." Iris adds, "Something you don't do is get up and drive somebody else's outfit. Every outfit is altogether different to drive. It just seems that way — you wouldn't do your best with somebody else's team, but Ron could. He could get up on any wagon there was in the whole circuit and drive them as good as anybody could drive them."

Reg also admired his dad's commanding ability to drive. "At the Calgary Stampede, Dad would go to the racehorse barns. He'd buy a horse, hook him in the morning, and hook him up again that night to race. His idea was that the horse would be so wired that first night that he'd get a little extra juice out of them. He had such total confidence about driving anything. It never bothered him."

Ron simply had a keen eye for horses. Iris reflects, "Ron was a great horseman. Ronnie could drive a horse once and know if he was a leader or a wheeler. He'd practice driving into the barrels, and he'd know by the way they stood or how their ears were perked if they were going to start good or not. He knew exactly what they were going to do and how they were going to do it."

Along with marketing his horses, Ron always put a little "action" on his enterprises. Tom states, "Dad was a wheeler-dealer, always betting with people. I think if he went a week without making a deal, it was pretty boring for him. He was always 'matching' with somebody. If he was having a beer or coffee or breakfast, he'd match you for it — like flip a coin to see who pays."

Ron was not reluctant to create certainty around his bets. "Dad always drove around in a truck with livestock racks on, in case he bought something — a cow, pig, or horse." Ron weighed his empty truck on the scales at High River's grain elevator. Tom adds, "He knew exactly what the truck weighed. When he'd buy a new horse at the racetrack, before coming home, he'd go to the elevator and weigh the truck and horse. Then he'd come home, and we'd break the horse, train it, whatever."

Several months later, Tom says, "We'd be at the wagon races, sitting in the barns with a beer. Tom Dorchester, Bill Greenwood — the old boys — would be sitting there in Dad's barn. All of a sudden Dad would look over and say, 'How do you like my new horse there? What do you think he'd weigh?' The guys would say, 'I don't know, Ron. Maybe eleven hundred pounds?' Dad would say, 'Aw, no, I think he's closer to twelve, and I'll bet you a bottle of whisky.'" Tom laughs, "Dad knew within twenty pounds what the horse weighed."

As a veteran of mischief, Ron kept a watchful eye on his teenaged children. Iris recalls, "If Reg stayed out late on Friday night and didn't come home when he was supposed to, on Saturday morning he and Ron went to work fixing fence. Ron would say, 'Come on, Reg, get your post-pounder. Let's go pound a few posts.'"

Reg remembers those early mornings. "When you're sixteen years old and partying to three in the morning, Dad's punishment was to get you up at six o'clock to go pound fence posts." On a third Saturday morning pounding posts, Reg showed his dad that he had broken the handle of his tool. "I didn't break it; I figured out how to hit it. If I hit the post-pounder at just the right angle and put on too much stress, I could pop the handle out. I did it two or three times. Finally, Dad had a pipe handle welded on." He laughs. "So much for that smartass."

Tom agrees. "Dad never hit any of us in his life, but if you were told to be home Friday night by ten, the next day, first thing in the morning, you'd hear that roar at the bottom of the stairs. You'd be cleaning the shit out of the chicken-house or in the field picking rocks. That was his way of doing it." He adds, "It never worked. We'd be late next Friday, too, because you forgot about it after a week."

Ron particularly watched Tara's comings and goings. Iris recalls, "On the nights Tara was a little late, she'd come in the front door. Before she could take her first step up the stairs, Ron would say, 'Bring me a glass of water, please, Tara.' He said that every time."

Tara laughs. "Dad always knew what time you got home, always. I don't think he ever drank the water, but he always asked for it."

Parties were a frequent attraction at the Glass farm. Reg says, "Once we got a little older, if there was a dance in the country, nobody went home. They all came here to party once the dance was over. Mom and Dad just went to bed and we'd keep partying. We've had some fantastic parties, no doubt about that." During the many parties, the boys got into a few dust-ups. Iris recalls, "The boys did fight. Somctimes they came home with black eyes." She told Rod, "Whenever anybody wants to fight, just turn and run. Get away from it. Don't fight."

But Rod replied, "Mom, I can't do that. My feet are so big, I can't run at all."

"I detest fighting," Iris states. "I just get wild when there is a fight." At one wagon show in Stettler, two young cowboys were about to fight behind the barns. "I told them, 'No, you're not fighting.' The guy said, 'Yes, we're going to fight.' I said, 'Well, if anybody's going to fight around this barn, it's going to be me.' I ran up and hit this guy right in the mush and knocked him right on his butt. I said, 'Now your mother did your fighting for you. Now go ahead and be embarrassed all you want, and get out of here.' They never did fight much around me, because they knew I'd get wild."

Unlike today, chuckwagon drivers were not then fined for fights in the barns. "So," Iris says, "you could hit anybody you liked. In the early days, they were tougher and rougher. Now they get a big fine — you can't touch anyone. Today, after a race, they still sass each other coming back off the track, where nobody can hear them — hollering and swearing and roaring. But they can't do it in the barns."

Although Ron was six feet, four inches tall and weighed 240 pounds, Reg says that what he remembers most about his father is his personality. "He was such a strong-minded character. He had kind of a force; everybody wanted to do something for him." For example, he says, "We'd go to town to buy horses at the track. Somebody would want $1,000 for the horse, and the old man would offer $300. He wanted the horse, big time, but he'd never let it show. He'd bullshit with the guy and eventually walk away, saying it was too much money. The guys never let him. Whatever he wanted to pay for it, they'd give it to him. People seemed to want to do things for him. They wanted to do what he wanted. It was a strange thing. I've never really seen that at work before.

"I think, without a doubt, he was the best at chuckwagons. Dad never won as many championships as other guys, but he never tried to. He won his championships early and then didn't really care about winning." Now, Reg says, "Drivers don't care what they pay for horses as long as they can win with them. Dad was the opposite. If you couldn't make money at what you were doing, it didn't make any sense to do it. He thought it was ridiculous if you couldn't win enough to pay back for what you'd spent." By the end of the wagon season, Ron would have sold all his best horses. "If he'd have kept the horses and tried to build stronger teams, I don't know how much he would've won — likely an incredible amount more. I could be a little biased, but I don't think much."

To his sons, Ron was never vocal with his praise, but he was quietly proud of them. Tom recalls, "During '80 and '81, I had a good outfit and we won the Battle of the Giants in High River. Dad was standing beside some stranger at the rail. Somebody told me that, after I won the race, he said, 'That's my son.' Later, Dad just shook my hand and said, 'Way to go.' That was a big thing from him. He wasn't into long congratulations and stuff. . . . I lost my dad right after that."

Ron Glass died of cancer at sixty-six, on September 3, 1981. Iris says, "He was not in the hospital long — that was the way for him to go. He still was a terribly strong man. They gave him so much dope that he didn't know where he was. That was the only way they could handle him."

In 1988 Ron was posthumously acknowledged as a Pioneer of Rodeo at the Calgary Stampede. In 1993 he was inducted into the Canadian Rodeo Historical Association Hall of Fame and, in 2000, into the Alberta Sports Hall of Fame, where a full-sized checkerboard wagon now rests.

But more memorable than his awards was the litany of wisecracks that Ron Glass bequeathed to his family. Reg says, "Dad was the master of one-liners. He wouldn't say anything for an hour and then just slide something in that was right on the money. Somebody would ask him about music and he'd say, 'Don't ask me. I can't even play the radio."

"Ron came up some of the damnedest cracks," Iris adds. "For example, he couldn't dance at all. We were at a party one night, and he was just a-giving 'er. He said, 'Oh boy, am I full of rhythm — because nothing has come out yet!' He'd say lots of things like that, and sometimes I didn't think he was a damned bit funny. I'd say, 'You're not funny.'" She smiles. "Ron would just laugh."

5

Your Mind in the Middle

My dad and brothers always told me,
"Start first and improve your position."
— IRIS GLASS

Chuckwagons were not the only things to gallop trophies into the Glass home. Success also came via the pony express. For many years, the Glasses and the Lauders were respected on Alberta racetracks for their jockeying talents. The women especially were superb riders.

When Iris was growing up, horse races were common. "As a kid," she recalls, "all you did was go fast, as fast as you could go. At home I practiced racing in the grain field. I never went slow in my life. I still don't go slow. I never let a horse walk — I've got to go faster. I always wanted to beat everybody. Oh boy, my sister Babe and I always tried to beat each other. Just to beat Babe was the greatest thing."

Even when they were riding to school, the Lauder girls would challenge each other. "We'd ride Dad's thoroughbreds to school and get the odd race going. Dad would say, 'No racing!' but we'd have to race. As if you rode a racehorse and couldn't race." When the Lauders lived at Pine Lake, Iris recalls, "We used to go and race around the nearby track to get a feeling for what that was like. We rode on jockey saddles with real short stirrups." She practiced standing in the stirrups at a gallop, learning how to enhance the rhythm of her horse, to move farther and faster.

For the chuckwagon shows, Tom Lauder always brought a racehorse for Iris to ride in half-mile or mile races. He advised her simply: "To ride a racehorse, put a leg on each side and your mind in the middle." Iris and her family raced mainly on the bush circuit, which encompassed the tracks in smaller communities outside of Calgary and Edmonton. "Trochu, Huxley, Lake McGregor — all the little towns had races on their fair days. The races were like running around home; I didn't think anything of it to get in a race and go."

Iris rode her first race in Ponoka at age ten and her last race at age fifty. She weighed 118 pounds for most of her career, and she and her sisters competed mainly against men. Flat racing was a male-dominated sport. One year, Iris and Babe tried to race at the famous July 1 Millarville Races (Millarville is between Calgary and High River). She recalls, "The big guys came out and said, 'You girls can't ride here.' We said, 'Why? We ride everywhere.' They said, 'Because the other jockeys in the paddock use very coarse language, and we don't want you ladies in there with them.'"

Iris retorted, "I bet I can out-cuss any one of them!" The next year, Iris, Babe, Mrs. Kenneth Buxton, and Miss Joanne Armstrong were among the racers. They were the first women to ride competitively at Millarville.

Iris won hundreds of horse races by being first off the starting line. The early races did not use a starting gate, so it was vital to jump out first and keep ahead of the early congestion. Tom Lauder emphasized, "You have to start first." If Iris could break away cleanly, then the other jockeys would have to catch her. "I did a lot of practicing lining up to start, to get to the front first. Two or three us would practice. You were supposed to walk your horses ahead to the start, but we'd practice getting our horses walking a little faster and a little faster, till you were a foot or two faster than the rest. Then they'd always say *Go!* and that'd be about it."

As she was nearing the starting line, Iris would inch ahead to the front. She laughs. "Before we had gates, the starters would tell us, 'Come line up here, guys. Ride up, now. Get in a line. . . . *Iris, get back!*' 'Yes, sir!' I'd say. But I always got the good start."

Babe Lauder chuckles, too. "It was really fun when my brother Bill, Iris, and I were in the same race. There might be three false starts. I think we went to eight false starts in Ponoka once, but we never did get ruled off."

With no starting gate, there was no limit to how many horses could be entered. Once gates were introduced, however, only eight horses were allowed in each race. Iris states, "None of us thought we'd ever like the gates. We had always been free to move this way and that way, and you were kind of caged. They were dynamite to go in. It was something, coming out of those gates the first time. Whew! It was scary to be locked in that steel thing, just the width of a horse. When the gate banged behind you, you thought, 'Oh my gosh.' Then the gate flew open, and, boy, those horses really went! We sure hung on when they left."

Iris smirks, "Guys always said, 'Boy, we're glad we've got these gates. Now Iris can't sneak up and get ahead of us.'"

When the race was under way, Babe Lauder says, "We rode tough. We knew we had good horses." But it wasn't always fun. For years the women did not wear goggles. As Babe describes, "Every now and then you'd get behind a horse that was a 'switcher.' That wasn't fun. The horse moved back and forth out of its lane, throwing crap at you. You didn't want to be behind on a dirty track!"

Iris stresses that the majority of races were, in fact, exhilarating and fun, but in a few instances their competitors challenged the women's skills. Since there were no video cameras, Babe says, "The idea was to get rid of the competition — hit you and knock you out of the game. Sometimes we were run into the rail. Other times, as I went riding by, the rider ahead whipped my horse's face. In Olds, I had one competitor beat on my leg with his stirrup for a quarter mile. I was on the outside of him, and he kicked my leg, trying to get my foot out of my stirrup. I won the race, but I couldn't walk — my leg was solid black."

During another incident, she explains, a guy cut her off in Cheyenne, and her horse fell. "I broke my shoulder and three ribs. It was all right — the horse did not get hurt, and the guy was ruled off the track for the next two or three days." Iris did not shy away from returning. "It was like when you were a little kid and you fell off. You're supposed to get right back on. I couldn't wait to get back on."

"We didn't love it when we got run off the track or beat on," Babe recalls. "But we didn't have to worry too much, since we had a lot of brothers and Ronnie."

Like Tom Lauder, Ron Glass had two or three racehorses that he took to the fairs. He also raced the family's wagon horses, which he would run in an afternoon quarter-mile, 5/8-mile, or one-mile race, and then race again with the wagon that evening. Interestingly, the quarter-mile race on quarter horses was more physically demanding than distance races on thoroughbreds. "It was the power in the quarter horse's shoulders; that's where your knees are locked," Babe explains. "The power went right through you. The majority of quarter horses also started way faster than a thoroughbred. You knew when you got off one that you'd been on a quarter horse."

Iris and her sister rode many outstanding horses. Trainers from the A circuit often brought their spoiled horses to "the bush." These were horses that would balk at going into the starting gates, or fight and rear up, straining not to step on the racetrack. The bush jockeys got the opportunity to ride the faster horses, and in return assisted with retraining the thoroughbreds.

Match races were common in the community. They were a means of cooling off a horse owner's hot air. Iris recalls, "We had dozens and dozens of match races. I was the jockey. We'd bet fifty or one hundred dollars, and I just loved to beat all those guys who thought they could beat our horses."

She recollects one particular match. "Some guy had a good racehorse in Saskatchewan. He won a race in the afternoon and walked the horse for half an hour, yapping and bragging. He got drinking, and Ron, who was quite a comedian, said, 'Good God, will you shut up for a while? I've got an old wagon horse over here tied to the truck that can outrun him.' Well, the guy just laughed and cackled, and said, 'When do you want to run?' 'Anytime,' Ron replied."

A hundred dollars was bet. "At that time a hundred dollars was a whole pile of money. We saddled the wagon horse, and I beat him by one hundred yards. The fellow took the horse back to the barns, he put him in a stall, took the saddle off, and shut the door. He never walked the horse at all. God, we laughed."

Iris emphasizes, "We always had a horse that could really run." The Glasses' famous lead wagon horse, Casey, also excelled in match races. At open starts (with no starting gate), Iris's competitors had little chance. "Casey stood right still, and when they said *Go!* he'd dig a hole six inches deep with his front feet, his shoes going. Man, would he start! I had to hang on to his mane as hard as I could with both hands or he'd throw me off backwards. My head was right down on top of my hands. He was the fastest-starting horse I've ever seen. The other riders never had a hope in hell after the first jump."

Another Glass horse, a half-thoroughbred named Flame, provided many thrills at the track. Iris says, "He was pretty snarly, but he was fast to start." He was so eager to start that Ron would hold his bridle and lead him onto the track. Iris would run alongside Flame, and her brother Jack would grab her foot and throw her on. "He got so bad that when I first got on him, he lunged and reared." Riding Flame one summer, Iris won every 5/8-mile contest they entered, nearly twenty-five races.

A constant air of unpredictability lurked on the racetrack. Sometimes, for example, the horses would choose a track of their own design. Babe recalls, "We had lots of horses duck out at the racetrack's entrance gate.

The horses don't forget where they came in. They're running around, and they think, 'That's the gate I came in' — and out they go. You try to pull on the reins, but there's a lot of power when they decide they're going straight home."

Iris recalls one afternoon when she rode a racehorse turned bronco. "I busted out first. We then had to go through the rodeo arena and around the track, but as we got into the arena, my horse just stopped and bucked me off. The cowboys said I didn't get any money, because I 'missed him out.' They all roared laughing."

In another incident, a horse Babe was riding swallowed its tongue. "They usually tied its tongue with a handkerchief to the side, but the owner forgot. That horse slowed down real quick. You can dig their tongue out before they choke on it, but meanwhile I was out in front of six or seven horses!"

Babe adds, "I was thrown in a race lots of times, but my first big wreck was in Airdrie, Alberta. Iris and I were there, and the rest of the family was in Ponoka. The first stinking race, I was out in front and we went down in a mudhole, a soft spot. I got up and the flesh from my jaw was all torn away from the bone — my chin sat on my chest bone. Mom and my sister- in-law Eileen didn't realize it was me when they came to the hospital."

Babe had one of her worst experiences when her stirrup hooked on the edge of a gate in Stettler. "It jerked the saddle off the horse. My foot luckily came out of the stirrup, but it was squished. I was hanging on the horse's side with a heel hooked over his hip. I was hanging underneath, and I was still out in front. I didn't want to fall in front of all those horses — I'd been there before — so I threw myself under my horse. It was pretty tense," she adds. "It didn't matter how you got hurt, you were back racing the next day or the next race. It was your job."

Not all of their racetrack adventures were caused by the horses. Sometimes elements on the racetrack were beyond the jockeys' control. At a race in Hand Hills, Alberta, Babe and Iris were racing side by side. Babe says, "We came around a corner and there was a woman in the middle of the track. We rode on both sides of her — we split and she spun like a top. When we were racing, it wasn't surprising to see people or a car on the track. Twice in Stettler there was a vehicle, and Hanna and Hand Hills were notorious for people on the track. They just didn't realize there was a race on."

Perhaps Babe's most frightening race occurred in Lethbridge, Alberta, when the tractor used to remove the starting gate stalled. "People were running up the track screaming, but we didn't know what they were screaming about. I came around the corner and the starting gate was on the track. I prayed a lot. I thought, 'Get the hell out of there! But if it's your turn, it's your turn.' I was sure glad my horse was neck-reined. I got him around the gate to the outside, and took another horse with me. The rest piled into the gate. It was a terrible wreck. After that, they started putting two tractors on a gate." Babe adds, "I have a picture of my horse and I trotting to the finish line. I thought, 'Well, hell, I'm still in the race. We're first.' And we trotted up."

Over so many years on the racetracks, Babe's and Iris's instincts kept them alive. "We'd get into some pretty tough binds," says Babe. "The horse breaks down. The horse has a heart attack. You get squished. You get knocked. You get run over. If you're not scared, you don't stay smart. You've got to respect the horses and appreciate them. If you want to live, be scared. But it can't affect you."

Iris agrees. "You wouldn't be human if you didn't get scared sometimes."

As jockeys, owners, and trainers, Iris and her family spent many memorable afternoons around the bush racetracks. In those prairie hippodromes they validated their horses' skills. They tested feed formulas, training programs, and new wagon horses. They raced for sport, for fun, and to let someone else eat their dust.

For Iris, the most memorable flat races were the ones won by two hundred yards. "You knew nobody was going to outrun you. It's nice to get way out in front, to show that you had the best horse. You don't give a damn about challenge if you can win a race by that far."

Among the hundreds of Iris's winning racehorses, Sparring Mate was a favorite. "When Sparring Mate ran a mile race, he'd be way behind after the first lap. Then he'd come from the back and win the race. You'd purdy near get sick, the first round. He wouldn't run; he'd just sit there galloping along. Then all of a sudden — *whoo!* — away he'd go!" During a race in Hand Hills, Iris's brother Jim was watching Iris and Sparring Mate from the rodeo corrals. "Sparring Mate and I were over a quarter-mile behind. Jim said to a friend, 'I bet you five dollars that the horse that's in the back will win this race.' The guy started to laugh and said, 'Aw, he'll never do that.' Jim said, 'Well, get out your money.' So he did, and we won."

6

Hard Mouths and Eager Hearts

When I sit on the wagon-box seat at a track or at the farm, and we leave the yard, I want those four horses to be paying attention to me, to my voice and the lines. I don't want to move one inch without all four horses being on the same page I'm at.
— JASON GLASS

From paddocks to racetracks, the Glasses' lives orbit around horses. The animals propelling the famous wagons have created the family's sense of worth. And their horseshoed partners are valued members of the extended clan. To really know the Glasses, you need to meet their horses.

It is unmistakable that horses command the Glass farm. The barn is redolent of flatulent geldings and urine-stained straw. The yard echoes with jingling chrome buckles and the slap of leather on wet horseflesh. Strong teeth crunch and munch in eagerly awaited pails of oats. Soft-lipped muzzles slurp from dented water troughs. Whipping tails send the maddening insects flying.

The Glasses can predict their horses' moods by the twitch and shift of chestnut-colored ears. The family jives with jittery leaders dancing towards the barrels. They relish the satisfaction of showering clean a sweat-lacquered wheeler. And they fly with the freedom of a thoroughbred's mane in a galloping breeze. The Glass farm is an equine commune.

"The horses get to be a part of the family," Iris says. "We love them all. If somebody came along and heard us all talking to the horses, they'd think us a little funny. But the horses do understand that we love them."

Cocksure, moody, eccentric, neurotic, bold, ambitious — literally thousands of horses have come through the High River farm. New horses arrive each year through flat racing and wagon racing. Most of them are thoroughbreds: hot-blooded, impassioned, and born to run. Edgy grenades hot to explode, these four-hoofed whirling dervishes are built for speed.

The Glass cowboys in their chuckwagons handle their horses ably. They make it seem effortless. Their deft touch, subtle movements, and confident stature make it look simple to control and drive four zealous thoroughbreds.

Jason Glass explains how easy it really is to drive four up. "Mel Gibson's stunt double [Mick Rogers] came out to the farm. He'd been around horses, driven a couple of teams, and he was kind of bragging to us how he could drive four-up." Jason joined his dad and Mick driving an outfit to the field. "It was late in the spring, when the horses were feeling good and strong. Dad said, 'Here you go,' and handed him the four lines. He was on a dead runaway in three seconds! He had no idea how strong the horses were and didn't expect it. We got the horses stopped, and it wasn't a big deal; the horses just knew that whoever had the lines didn't know what they were doing. They have a bit in their mouth, and it's a pretty sensitive area. It doesn't take much for a horse to understand who has control or not."

While they were unhooking the team, a horse head-butted Mick, chipping a couple of his teeth. Jason recalls, "This guy had kind of a rough day. He came here and thought it was no big deal — that it was really easy to do and to be around. In one day, he had a runaway and broke some teeth. That kind of thing happens to people who think it's that easy and anyone can do it. There is a lot of power."

Since Ron Glass's era, the Glasses have used thoroughbred geldings to pull their wagons. These horses arrive from the racetrack, where they can no longer run competitively. The burden of carrying a jockey's weight injures horses to the point where they cannot flat race. Pulling a wagon gives them a second chance.

Iris states, "We've had dozens of horses that had bad legs and were brought home. After a year off, they'll run for years on the wagon. I think the atmosphere of the racetrack must be hard on them. They're never out of the barn except to go around the track, and here they're so free. Not being pressured does a lot of healing, too."

Iris brought home many of the family's horses, often towing a new horse home after spending a day at the races. One day, she brought Fred home. "I put him in the back of the barn. Ron said, 'A new horse, eh?' I said, 'Yes, I bought that new horse. I paid a thousand dollars for him, and I want eleven hundred. I want to make a hundred dollars.' I told Ron, 'Now, don't touch him. You're not driving him till you pay me.'

"He never said much about that. About a week later, I went to town to do something. I was there all day, and when I came back there was a cheque on the table. I said, 'Oh, you decided to buy that horse? So you want to drive him?' Ron said, 'I already did, and he's going to make a leader.'" Iris laughs, "Ron only drove him once, but he knew how the horse took the bit and how he would do. He was pretty sneaky like that."

During spring training, the Glasses harness rookie horses with old draught horses. The new horse must become comfortable with the hanging harness, the collar, and the sensation of pulling rather than carrying. Iris says each horse is "taken really slow, because there is a lot for them to learn. It's quite a science to get it all worked out — we have a few runaways. It gets quite exciting here in the spring." When the boys are out in the field with fresh horses, Iris is prepared for a potential wreck. She stands ready by the open gate with two spare halter ropes and a halter shank.

Iris also helps train new outriding horses. She rides them in the field, where she has no worries about running into something. Occasionally, she does find herself on top of a runaway thoroughbred: "I've always said, 'I can ride as fast as you buggers can run.' So I just go to it."

Nervous new wheel horses sometimes kick at the wagon box or the doubletrees. Ron Glass had a simple solution to stop their kicking. "If a wheeler wanted to kick, Ron tied its tail to the leather tug with a piece of string. A horse won't kick unless he can switch his tail." Another trick to prevent a horse from kicking is simply to lift a front foot off the ground — a horse will not kick from only three feet.

When new horses are being broken to race, sometimes they will balk at the starting horn. They simply plant their feet and do not move. Tom says, "You can't do anything. I've seen guys take a buggy whip and smack them on the ass. The horse's ears roll back and they just plant themselves harder." Tom remembers watching his dad sit out in the yard for an hour with a balky horse. "He just sat there and sat there. We came out after breakfast, and he was still sitting there. Pretty soon that horse turned his head back and looked at Dad. Then he lifted one foot and put it back. After an hour, the horse thought, 'Geez, this is boring.' Then he fidgeted and moved. Pretty soon, away he went. The horse took himself out of it. He decided not to stand there anymore, just like he decided to stand there in the first place.

"When you let them take themselves out of it, they probably won't do it anymore, but not if you beat them out of it. There are two ways to train a horse, either kindness or abuse. In my experience, abuse will work for a day, but overall it'll beat you. They've got to want to do it. They've got to want to start. They've got to want to go. It's no different than kids. You see guys that slap their kids around. Well, what do you end up with? You've screwed them for life. I've never lifted a hand on my kids, and my kids pretty well do anything I've ever asked them. They do it out of respect for me. I've earned that from them."

Working with horses is a psychological conundrum. The Glasses must unravel each horse's unique personality. They then try to determine what position in the outfit is best for it. Finally, they must combine three other horses to work cooperatively with that horse. The horses' personalities, characteristics, and temperaments are all factors in the chuckwagon puzzle.

For Jason, getting inside a horse's head is his favorite element of the sport. It begins when he brings horses home in the winter. "I go out to the corral each day. I walk around with them. I put them into different pens. I move them around a little bit. I try to figure out what they're all about. Some will be strong and push other horses around the corral. Others are wimps, and they're the last ones to get into their oat buckets. All that seems to matter in the long run with a horse. Some people don't think any of that makes a difference, but it's all part of their character and their personality."

In order to unite his team, Jason offers his horses respect. In the barns he communicates positively, so the horses will respond positively to the messages he transmits through the lines. Jason explains his approach. "For me, to drive a wagon — from the very first second you're ever around a horse till the end of any race — every second is important. You've got to get those horses comfortable and liking what they're doing, or it's not going to work. You're dealing with horses that have got to respond from your hands, through the lines and the bits in their mouths. If you want four horses to cooperate, to be completely comfortable and do well for you, you've got to find a way to get along with them through the lines. That's probably the most difficult thing for any driver."

Jason feels that the failure to do this explains why some thirty-year veteran drivers rarely place in the top ten. "Even guys who have been driving for ten, twenty years — there are some guys who have never figured out what works for them. One way or another, you've got to be a team, right down to the guys that work for you in the barn."

In selecting horses for their ideal wagon team, the Glasses seek thoroughbreds with "hard mouths." Iris explains: "The hard-mouth horses are the ones who really get a hold of their bits and pull on their lines. They are the horses who really bow their necks and go." Horses learn to run into their bits at the racetrack. "Racehorses run [with] balance," explains Reg. "That's partly why they can run as fast as they do. Their balance increases their stride. When you train a racehorse, you train him into the bit. When he's pushing into the bit, it locks up a line of muscle and bone extending from the jaw over top to the croup." This locked line balances the horse. "All racehorses have very strong mouths, some more than others. They all have to take hold of the bit, or they can't run. If it's loose, they have no balance."

Lead horses specifically must charge into their bits for control and power. "The wheelers are tied to the wagon," Tom describes, "and they go where the wagon goes, but your lead team are loose, and they flop around. You can't push them with the lines. They've got to want to go somewhere."

Similarly, when the Glasses talk about "mouth," they refer to how much pull a horse has on the lines. The amount of mouth can make the difference between success and a wreck. "The biggest way to get in trouble is at the start of a race," Reg explains, "when an old lead team starts looking at the top barrel. They get up there, and they want to turn early. If your right-hand leader is not taking the bit in his mouth and pulling, you're sitting there with a wet noodle — the driver has no control of the horse. The horse runs up, flops back early, and the team runs over the barrel." During the race, the drivers hold their lines tight to the horses' mouths. The only time they offer slack is when the horses turn off of the bottom barrel. Iris says, "Then you give the horses all the line they need. You send them a message to *go!*"

Curiously, when the lines are held tight, the horses run more swiftly. According to Iris, "It is like when you were a little kid and you could run just so fast, but if somebody hung on to your hand, you could run faster. That's the same with a horse's mouth. If the horse can take hold of the line, they'll run faster, because the line is holding their mind and heart up." When she was riding racehorses, Iris ensured that she held her horse's head up with a tight line. "God help you if you had a slack or loose line. You got told about it."

As a consequence, the Glasses are very protective of their horses' mouths. "Ron was a very quiet man who did not raise a hand to one of his children," Iris relates. "And when it came to horses, Ron had no patience for mishandling and abuse. Ron said, 'You can never hit a horse. You can't pound on them. They've got to like you if they're going to run for you.' If you were leading a horse to a pasture and you jerked their bit — *whoo,* would he get mad! He'd yell, 'Don't you ever touch that horse's mouth like that ever again! If you want to tell the horse something, slap him in the butt or kick him in the belly, but don't you ever touch their head. They win their money from their mouth. The horse's mouth is a very special thing.'"

The Glasses face significant hurdles in creating and maintaining a fast-starting team. "The hardest thing about wagon racing," says Tom, "is keeping a horse from getting over-intelligent. That's the whole key to winning wagon races." For example, "the wheelers are hard to keep starting all the time, because they get smart. They begin thinking, 'I jump, hit that collar, and pull that wagon. Why the hell do I need to do that? I'll just stand here.'" After three or four years of racing, most wheelers will refuse to start powerfully.

For Tom Glass, the most difficult horse to find is a right-hand leader. "That horse has got to go straight up, past the barrel, turn straight back into himself, and go the other way as hard as he can. A thoroughbred horse is never bred to do that. They're bred to come out of a starting gate and run as fast as they can in one direction, around in a circle. They're not bred to just stand there with nothing holding them. It's a hard thing breaking a horse to just stand. Just think of what you're asking a high-spirited horse. You feed him vitamins, five gallons of oats a day, the best hay in the world, and you put him in a box stall. He's full of energy. Next, you hook him on a wagon and warm him up so the blood is just pumping. Then you ask him to walk out in front of 20,000 people and stand perfectly still for four or five seconds after you've pumped and warmed him up. It's amazing they do it!

"And then, when that horn blows, you ask him to leave there as hard as he can, to give everything he's got — jump and go straight ahead for fifty feet, stop, turn around, go the other way, and turn again. If you think about it, in their minds it's got to be, 'Wow, what does this guy want me to do?'

"That's the easy part. The hard part is when you're training him every day. You take him by the barrel and turn him back, so he knows how to do it. All of a sudden, when he gets halfway up there, he starts going for the barrel. That's a sign of intelligence. That horse knows he's going to go up there and turn to the right, so why the hell doesn't he start early? Why wait? He starts cheating on you. They're smart. Pretty soon you've got the greatest leader in the world, and you can't get him by the barrel. You can pull all you want, but he can still cheat with his body. It's not that the horse gets old, hurt, or too slow; it's that they get too smart. Soon he's what we call a 'sour leader.'"

Tom recalls a ploy his father used to out-anticipate his horses. "My dad was the first guy I saw do it, and I did it a few times after. He'd pull into the barrels on his practice turn, and when the horse started to go right, he'd turn to the left — the wrong way. People in the stands would say, 'What the hell is Glass doing? Can't he drive?'" But Tom affirms, "A horse shouldn't go anywhere until you put them there. The next time, the horse wouldn't make that move to the right. It worked a few times, but the horses are intelligent, and they know that when the race is on they're going to the right." When the leaders become too smart to drive, they rejoin the team as outriding horses.

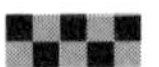

Among the Glass family, the wagon-racing community, and horse lovers all over, barn fires are a terrifying nightmare. The hay and dry kindling in old barns can ignite quickly, suddenly turning a quiet pastoral scene into a flaming panic.

In 1974 there was a fire in the Calgary Stampede's horse barns. Iris recalls, "It was the most horrid thing I ever went through." That evening's wagon races had been completed, and Tom and his friend Richard Cosgrave had gone to the Ranchman's Bar. Iris was visiting friends behind the wagon barns, when "all of a sudden somebody screamed 'Fire! Fire!' I looked down, and a barn was really burning." There were two barns between the blaze and the barn where Tom's horses were stabled. Tom's children were asleep in a trailer parked beside the Glass barn.

Iris shudders. "You couldn't go near the burning barn. It was pitch dark, except for the lights over the barns. And then about four horses started running; whoever got into the barn had turned them loose. Some of their tails and manes were on fire. You had to hide behind something as they ran through all the barns. They scared you. Then you had to run to your barn to see if the horses dropped anything that could burn — to see if part of their tail fell off or something. The horses were just terrified. You knew they could start a fire, but you couldn't catch them. One hundred cowboys were trying to catch them. It was a noisy, wicked place for a few hours."

Iris found a telephone. "I phoned the Ranchman's and told the girls, 'Tell Tom to come home. Tell him to come to the grounds right away, but don't say anything about a fire, because we have a real tragedy. Don't say anything about that.' But before he got ready to go, somebody told him."

Without knowing whether his horses were hurt, Tom sped back towards the grounds. In his haste, he T-boned another car at an intersection, breaking his arm in the accident. The policeman who came to the scene was not a horseman and did not appreciate Tom's concern. Alarmed and distressed, Tom was taken by the police to the hospital.

When he finally got back to the barns, he learned that his family and horses were unhurt. "They finally got the fire down," Iris says. "They kept barrel-racing horses and Stampede rodeo pickup horses in the end barn.

Two barrel horses were killed." She adds flatly, "The next day, I couldn't go near the barn to see what horses they took out or anything that burned."

The adoring rapport between the Glasses and their horses is founded on years of shared experiences. Their common ordeals have built relationships filled with compassion and respect. In 2000 Jason began building a forgiving friendship with a horse named Firebird. The horse was named for a patch of white hair above his front leg. "It looks exactly like a bird with its wings out," Iris says, "like a seagull flying." When Firebird arrived at the Glass farm, he had a bowed tendon, an injury requiring time and rest to heal. Jason put him in a box stall, and for three months Jason and Reg's wife, Jeanne, took special care of the horse.

When Firebird was looking healthier, Jason decided to move him. "Firebird had only been out of his stall to have his feet trimmed," he recalls, "but I didn't have trouble, so I thought I'd be fine. I had a chain around his nose, because I was taking him from one barn to the other. I got him about ten feet outside the barn when he just reared up and started striking at me with both feet." Jason was wearing a heavy work coat with deep front pockets. "The horse stuck his foot right into a pocket. There was no way it was coming out, so he kept striking at me."

The horse gave a lunge backwards and Jason's feet went out from under him. As he fell, the horse's hoof ripped off the coat pocket. Firebird jumped over Jason and ran away. If the hoof had not come free, he might have landed right on top of Jason. "I was just trying to hang on to the shank. I thought if I let it go, he'd be running somewhere. I didn't really care that he had me underneath him. I just didn't want to let him go, because two months was down the drain as soon as he went running."

The horse ripped the shank out of Jason's hand, panicked, and galloped down the lane towards the highway. The distressed animal was running and falling into ditches. "We were able to cut him off in a truck," Jason says, "and finally get him headed back up the lane. It was kind of my own fault. I should've had a couple of halter shanks on him and a couple of extra guys. But the horse had been pretty good, and I just never expected it."

Among the thousands of race- and wagon horses the Glasses have healed and trained, a few stand out prominently. These horses were true partners, friends, and accomplices in their mutual ambition to race and win. A large sorrel wheeler named Mike was one of these special horses. Initially, Mike was destined for the cannery, because he'd run into a fence while playing in a field and badly lacerated his hock. The horse was hobbling, with a cut and swollen leg, and Ron decided to take him to "the can." He tried to load Mike into the back of his truck, but the horse valiantly and insistently refused. Finally, Ron gave up and turned Mike loose in the pasture with the other horses.

Tom says, "It was the only time I'd ever seen my dad not finish what he set out to accomplish. I figure he may have only been trying half-hearted." Appropriately, Mike's racetrack name was Remain Alive.

After his reprieve, big Mike evolved from being very aggressive and difficult to control into one of the best wheelers the Glasses have owned. "Mike had so much power," says Tom. "He knew any second that horn would go, and he had to leave. He'd anticipate the horn and start ahead of the gun. We'd get in trouble, have a false start, and come back."

"He was the startingest horse we ever owned," agrees Iris.

Tom describes Mike's unique talents: "With our lead teams, when you put a wheel team behind them, they'd usually stand there pretty good. But when you brought out Mike to hook up, the leaders would know. Just about the time you'd get to hooking them, they'd be wanting to get out of there, because they knew when Mike left, he left hard."

Mike was partnered with an equally gifted horse named Dale. "We drove Dale for twelve years," Iris says, "and there wasn't one day he refused to start. When the horn blew, he jumped so hard that, if you weren't hanging with the lines, he'd throw the driver back off the seat." Mike and Dale motivated the whole outfit. Tom says, "If we had a lead team that even just got out of their way, we were going to *go* to the racetrack, 'cause they're gone."

Iris laughs. "Mike was just like a big kid. He could open every barn door and every gate. He walked around like he owned this farm. At the shows, we'd make corrals with poles and two parallel ropes. Mike would stick his head between the ropes and his feet over the bottom. Mike would stand there with the fence open till Dale got out, and away they would go."

In Jason's corrals, Kurt Cobain is one of his most treasured horses. He says, "Reg was snooping around the racetrack in Calgary, and he brought home two horses for me. They were cheaper, kind of average horses, and really had not won very much. One horse was just kind of nuts. You'd walk in the barn and he'd step on you, kick you, or run you over. He had no respect for people." Jason's roommate decided that Kurt Cobain was a suitable name for this rebel horse.

The first day Jason hooked Kurt Cobain on the wheel, he recalls, "He didn't try to run away, but he was full-bore straight ahead. He didn't care that he was hooked to a wagon or that there was harness on him. The next day we hooked him in the lead, and today I still drive him on the right-hand lead. He's a natural horse, but he's still got the attitude that he doesn't care about people around him."

During one racing season, Jason noticed that Kurt Cobain's right eye was becoming blurry. He tried to heal it with drops and medication, but the eye became foggier and foggier. Finally, "I took him to the vet clinic, and they eventually had to remove the eyeball and nerves out of his right eye." The next spring, Kurt Cobain seemed healthy, and Jason started driving him again. He drove him until July, even though the horse had only one eye. "We got to Ponoka, and his left eye had an ulcer in it. I took him back to the vet clinic, and he was there for about two months with a patch over the only eye he had. It finally cleared up. I brought him home, gave him the whole winter off, and the next year I used him again.

"He's one of my favorites, for sure. He went through a lot. He's tough, he doesn't care, and does his job. He seems to like what he's doing, and he's liked it right off the bat. He's his own horse and his own personality. Even in the corrals he doesn't really buddy up with other horses. Most of them are sucks — they've got to buddy up. They find a friend and you can't separate them. But Kurt Cobain's a horse that's never been that way. He just does his own thing."

At the Glass farm, every horse, sick or healthy, requires a 365-day commitment. Tom describes that commitment: "People don't realize the work in it. During spring it's like having a class of twenty-five kids, only they don't go home from school — you've got them. You get up in the morning, and it doesn't matter if it's Saturday, Sunday, or what day it is, there are twenty-five of them out there needing feeding and their shoes fixed. They need to be driven, and they need to be exercised, every day, seven days a week.

"Even in the winter, when they're out on pasture, [the work's] not done. They still have to be fed, they have to have their feet done, their teeth done, and they need de-worming. They never go away; they're there all the time. It's nice, but there are times when you say, 'Hell, I'm going on a holiday. Look after them for me.' But when you get back, usually there's something to look after. It's a big job.

"There's always one of them that hurt their leg or bumped their knee. And ninety percent of the time they do it in the corral, playing. It's not on the racetrack." Tom lost Carrufer, a favorite leader, to a freak accident in a field. "I had no idea how he did it. Somehow he stumbled, flipped over, landed, and broke his back, right out in the middle of a wide-open space. I've had more horses hurt in the field, or out in a corral with good fences, than on the racetrack."

And yet, despite all the time the horses demand, the Glasses are indebted to their piebald partners. Iris says, "When Tom won Calgary for Totem [Hardware], they had a great big supper. People asked, 'Where's Tom?' and I'd say, 'He's in there telling his horses how good they were.' I think he made seven trips to talk to them and give them a pet."

With such an investment of time, money, and love, it is no wonder that tempers flare when a horse is hurt in a wagon race, particularly if the injury is inflicted by someone's reckless driving. "It makes you mad when somebody hurts your horse," states Iris. "The horses are your whole life in chuckwagon racing. They are everything."

Iris recalls an incident when a competitor crowded Tom's outfit in a Regina race. Tom's horse's foot was run over, tearing its hoof. "I was going to give [the guilty driver] a licking," Iris growls, "but he wouldn't get off the wagon. He just sat up there and laughed at me, so I was really mad. So I swore a whole bunch at him." She adds, "They brought it up at a meeting that I was swearing in the barn and I should be fined. They eventually threw it out, but I get pretty mad sometimes.

"Those horses, when you hitch them up, they run just as hard as they can, with all their heart. They do the very best that they know how, and when somebody hurts them, it just gets you. Oh boy, oh boy, the drivers get mad when they're hurt. Some guys, you know, can't drive, but when a good driver hits a horse there's no excuse whatsoever."

To reduce accidents, there are now chalk lines on the track, delineating where the cowboys must drive when coming off the barrels. Before the lanes were set up, wagons often collided and horses were hit. Iris says, "The horses would get their legs in the wheels. It was bad, so now the lines are there to stop them from doing it."

Accidents are still caused by drivers falling out from the rail. Iris explains: "You've got to keep your eyes working in the back of your head when you're wagon racing. If you're not hanging on to the horses' heads, they will drift out from the rail. You've got to have your eyes going in every direction when you're in something that fast and so many things are around you. You've got to always be looking."

Penalty times are assessed to drivers who crowd and bang horses. Yet, Iris wonders, "What good is a penalty? A penalty means you don't get as much money, but it doesn't do the horse any good." She admits, "It's a very, very dangerous sport — really dangerous — with four wagons and thirty-two horses that go as fast as they do. With the adrenaline and the speed, it's wonderful there haven't been more accidents. It's a small place for all of them to stay in their right place. But that's the thrill of wagon racing."

When horses are injured, animal-rights protesters confront the chuckwagon community, trying to shut down their sport. The Glasses, with their high public profile, have been particularly vulnerable to activists and their complaints. Iris says, "I'll hear people talking and I'll yell, 'What's that? Do you know *anything* about chuckwagons and horses? Do you know a damn thing at all?' Then they just look around. 'Oh dear. Oh gosh.' But they don't know what it's all about. To those who say chuckwagon racing is cruel to horses, I say, 'Just come around and I'll show you how it isn't.'"

Without wagon racing, the majority of these high-strung gelded thoroughbreds would be sent to the cannery. With it, they are offered a longer, richer, fuller life. Iris affirms, "These horses are born to run. They are bred to run. They love to run. You can tell as soon as you hitch them up that they love it."

One evening, the Society for the Prevention of Cruelty to Animals visited the Glass barn at the High River races. Tom went into a stall and brought out Dale. Iris recounts, "Tom said, 'You see this horse? I drove him for twelve years on the wheel of this wagon. How does he look to you?' They said, 'Oh, he looks beautiful. He looks simply beautiful.' Tom said, 'Well, that's how long I've driven him.' Tom took Dale back to the barn, and the SPCA went home."

When the cowboys are charged with being callous and cavalier towards their animals, it is clear their accusers have not been in the barn when a horse is injured. For example, in Edmonton, Jason lost a horse named Remington. "I bought him off my dad. He was a crazy bastard, but a very nice horse — an irreplaceable right-hand leader. He didn't care anything else but about doing his job." Jason had made the final heat: the Dash for Cash. As they were coming around the third corner, Remington broke his leg and fell down.

"I lost him. That was one of the toughest things I've gone through. There's a horse of mine, running his heart out to win a race for me, and you lose him just like that — *snap*! He kind of died right in my arms, too. It was a shocker. You don't think you're that attached to them until something like that happens, and then you go, '*Ho-ly* shit.' Those things hurt, but I guess they just make you stronger, and you carry on somehow. I cried that night for sure.

"The horses work so hard for you, and you've got to put so much into them to get anything back out. Compared to a dog, who is a companion, these horses are part of our lives and our jobs. That's probably why you get that much more attached to them. When I get up in the morning, I'll make sure those horses are fed or doctored before I feed myself. You're so concerned with those horses that you become second to them. For me, I know it's a downfall in terms of a family or, say, a girlfriend. Everything else always seems second to those horses. But if it wasn't for those horses, I wouldn't have this house; I wouldn't have anything. It'd be a definitely different ball game."

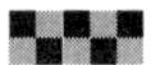

Ultimately, either through injury or age, horses retire from wagon racing. Iris says, "When they quit running, if the horse is not lame or sick, we turn them out and let them stay till they're unhappy." In the winter, the horses are pastured and given hay every day. But, Iris says, "They don't care much for being free. When they're over in the big field and you go to the fence, they'll come over wanting to be talked to and petted. The boys do that all the time. The horses don't like it where there aren't any people. They depend on you to be a friend."

When they begin to suffer, the horses are euthanized. Iris recalls one incident. "Tommy can't take them to where the horses are put down, so Jason thought he would do it. He took two horses; one was lame, and one had a very bad foot. Jason took a five-gallon pail of oats, waited till they ate the oats, and then told the guy he could put them to sleep. Jason came back and said, 'I'll never do that again. Don't you guys ever, ever ask me! I won't. You can hire somebody to do it.'" A hired man now transports the horses. Iris emphasizes, "There's not a soul in this yard when the horses are being taken away. The ones you love are hard to lose."

But lost horses are never forgotten. The Glasses remember and continue to cherish their chuckwagon partners through the images strewn about their homes. These are enduring relationships. Often the first subjects the Glasses recognize in a wagon photo are the horses. And the ages of family members are remembered by which horses they had at the time. Horses embody their memories of time and of place. Horses have been their allies in everything that the Glasses have achieved. Echoing his grandmother, Jason Glass declares in heartfelt tones, “I owe everything to a horse. I don’t have a problem saying that, either.”

7

Destined to Chew Wagon Dust

We grew up in this kind of life. It's like a race-car driver. We did what our parents did, and when you grow up doing it, you kind of rule out the danger. It's normal. Where other people think we're crazy or brave, it's not necessarily that.
— REG GLASS

Reg Glass, Ron and Iris's eldest son, was raised amid kicking horses, Ferris wheels, jangling doubletrees, and corn dogs. "When Reg came into a rodeo grounds," Iris recalls, "he'd look over, see the grandstand, and say, 'We're home, Dad.'" Reg feels that fate shone upon him — he had a special childhood. He feels it was "a kid's dream come true to grow up in this kind of family. People move so fast these days, but for us every weekend was another rodeo, and we went in a couple of days ahead of time."

Reg recalls a show in Cheyenne, Wyoming, where trainer Glen Randall, who supplied horses for Roy Rogers and other movie cowboys, had his horses next to the Glass barn. One night, Reg and a High River friend sneaked into Randall's barn and rode all the horses. "We might be the only kids from Canada ever to ride Trigger and Koko [Rex Allen's horse]," Reg recounts. "It was a tremendous way to grow up — a little adventure and a little excitement. And when I was a teenager, it was even better. At the rodeo dances every night, girls were looking for a cowboy."

When he wasn't dancing, Reg was busy racing; his parents made sure of that. "You ended up in every damn event there was to enter: cart races, chariot races, and relay races. And we often were 'over-mounted' — trying to play some kid's game on a thoroughbred that was off the racetrack for only a month."

Reg regularly rode his dad's thoroughbreds in relay races. The relay rules were simple. Each rider circled the track three times on three different horses. The riders started with one horse and one saddle, raced around the track, switched the saddle to another horse, hopped on him, ran around, and then jumped on the third one. Ron and Iris held his spare horses on the track while Reg raced. To exchange saddles quickly between horses, Reg tied the saddle cinch loosely. "We just put the cinch through one time and wrapped it around the saddle horn." Riding with a loose saddle on a fresh horse, it was a challenge to stop the steed and still keep the saddle on. Reg says, "I had quite a bit of trouble with that." He avoided the problems of pulling up his horses by pointing them at his father. "With the size of Dad, I just aimed the horse at him. He just reached out and grabbed him. That was it — you weren't going anywhere."

Reg stresses that during the relays, "When you raced with Mom and Dad helping you, you were damn sure goin' out to win. I'd throw the saddle on; they'd throw the lines and yell *hyaw!* Sometimes I didn't have a dally, I didn't have the lines, but I was gone." With his parents' able assistance, Reg won Cheyenne's relay races twice.

Back at the farm, Ron also expected his son to be able to handle any horse. Reg recalls, "He'd send me out with four horses across the road and into the field. I'd be scared to death, but Dad wouldn't even watch. He'd go back into the barn while I was gone. Dad never told you too much," he adds. "He wasn't much of a teacher. He just thought if you had a problem, you'd learn from it. He always had total confidence that you could handle whatever he put you into. His attitude was, you should just be able to do it. 'You want to learn? Watch.'"

Spring was a term of education for Reg. Runaways were, and still are, a seasonal rite at the Glass farm. Ron told Reg that, when his horses start charging, he should simply turn them in a circle. "The chuckwagons are already rough to ride in," Reg declares, "but when they get running away on you and you're bouncing over the field, just trying to stay on the wagon is hard enough. One time, to keep them fit, I was driving a couple of Dad's friend's racehorses. They were really, really hard-mouthed horses. I took them in the field out behind the barn, and I just couldn't drive them. They'd start to run away on me, and I'd crank them in a circle. As soon as I'd straighten them out, they'd go again.

"Dad was fixing fence right by where I was driving. Dad didn't like you giving up too much, but I got over there and said, 'You've gotta take these horses.' He replied, 'Aw, go on, you're all right.' I said, 'No! I can't!' Finally, I came by the fence, and as soon as I straightened them out I yelled, 'Goddam it, you've gotta take these. You've gotta take them.'"

Reg laughs, "So then he's mad. He throws the hammer down, he jumps into the cart and goes *ppfff* [a kissing sound], and throws the lines away. Those horses just tore out of there and ran off on him. Dad goes to crank them — rolls the cart over, driving his head into the summer fallow field. His mouth and eyes were full of dirt. I couldn't stop laughing. I was all wired up anyway about having to make Dad drive and him being mad at me for that. So the tension just kind of released. Dad came up, spitting out dirt. He looked at me with a big smile and said, 'Well, come on. You can at least help me catch them.' And away we went."

As a competitor, Reg drove the smaller, pony chuckwagons; he did not drive the thoroughbreds professionally. "It wasn't that Dad tried to discourage me about driving, because for quite a few years I did most of the driving in the spring, breaking new horses and getting them fit." Although he substituted for drivers in a couple of races (once for Gordie

Bridge), Reg admits, "To tell you the truth, I don't know why I didn't drive. I had to do a lot of driving in the spring, when it was cold, and it just wasn't a big thing for me to drive. It's something I just never bothered doing. Dad definitely didn't think we should be wagon drivers. When we were kids, there wasn't much money in wagon racing. Even when Tommy started, Dad did everything he could to discourage him."

Tom agrees. "Dad never at all encouraged me. He used to say quite regularly, 'Get a job. There's more money in it than wagon racing.' But I never listened to him; I just kind of kept going at it. I never got very serious for the first while. I was more having a good time — I did a lot of living before I was twenty."

Ron's reluctance to encourage his sons stemmed from his own experience. Iris suggests, "At age fourteen or fifteen, the boys wanted to drive. Ron started at that age, too, and he remembered how tough it was for him. So he always told the boys to wait. He told them, 'You can practice here, but wait.'"

Ron believed his sons should pursue higher education rather than wagons. Reg says, "Dad really thought highly of education and a decent career. All the time we were going to school, he tried to aim us that way. I just think he wanted us to do something that he considered better." But, despite Ron's prodding, the horse-centered life was too ingrained. Stallions, mares, colts, and fillies were entrenched in the family's heritage. They would steer Reg's career as well.

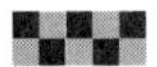

At age eighteen Reg Glass earned a degree with a difference while working for Buddy Heaton. Big, brash Buddy Heaton was a caricature from the Wild West. Originally from Kansas, he was a buffalo-riding rodeo clown and a businessman who imported Mexican merchandise. "Heaton was as famous as Slim Pickens across North America," says Reg. "Kids followed him by the dozen. He was six feet, three inches tall, with long hair, and looked like the wrestler Bret Hart. He had a reputation for being the craziest man in the world." During rodeos, for example, "after a bull had bucked off its rider, Buddy would jump off the fence onto the bull's back. 'Yahoo!' He'd ride till the bull threw him off, too."

The first time Reg remembers meeting Buddy Heaton was in a barn in Cheyenne. "It was raining to beat hell, and in comes Heaton. My old man had had a couple of drinks, and he says to Buddy, 'Let me try them boots.' Heaton sits down, takes his cowboy boots off, gives them to Dad, and Dad throws them on. Dad had broken both his feet and had great big insteps. So Dad says, 'They're too tight!' Dad pulls out his jackknife and cuts a hole across these ostrich-skin boots. He says, 'Yeah, they fit all right.' Heaton says, 'Goddam you, Glass,' and walks away in his sock feet. I thought Heaton was going to kill him when he stuck the knife in the boot. They were a $300 pair of boots, when a $100 pair was the best you could buy. After Heaton went away, Dad says, 'They're too tight,' and tosses them to me. I got the slits sewn up and wore them for years."

Reg worked for Heaton for two years at his ranch in Midnapore (now a south Calgary suburb). He recalls, "It was the wildest experience you'd ever seen. We'd sit at his place watching Calgary pro wrestling on TV. At that time all the wrestlers lived in apartments across from the Stampeder Hotel on Macleod Trail. Heaton would say, 'That so-and-so ain't so tough.' We'd drive up to the Stampeder to try and find the wrestlers, pick a fight with them, give them a roughing up, and go back home again."

But wrestlers were not Heaton's only punching bags, Reg says. "While I worked for him, Heaton gave me a couple of lickings, too. One day, we were practicing steer wrestling. If you missed your steer, the next guy just came in. All kinds of guys were missing. It was my turn, and Heaton says, 'Now, wait till I'm ready.' So I look over, and he looks ready, so I nod for the steer. Down I go, and Heaton did not come."

Reg didn't think anything was unusual. He let the steer go and walked his horse out of the arena. "As I tied my horse to the fence, Heaton came charging up and yelling, 'I told you to goddam wait till I was ready.'" Reg laughs. "That wasn't what he said, but I couldn't care less. I said, 'Fine, whatever.' Heaton spins me around and says, 'You little punk. I'll teach you to pout.' And he backhands me about six goddam times across the face. He rips my shirt. I didn't even know what the hell was going on. He knocks my face into a smile, then stops, and yells, 'Aw, you think it's funny, do you?' I said, 'You crazy son of a bitch. Let go of me.' I wasn't mad, but it was just straight out of the blue. I got out of there and went up to his house to pack my stuff and leave."

Buddy came into the house to find Reg. As he was coming up the stairs, Reg says, "He gave me a box of twelve western shirts. Then he reached in his pocket and gave me $400, which was a hellacious amount of money, and the keys to the newer pickup. Heaton says, 'Here, take a week off — go spend the money, get drunk, have fun. Forget about this. Come on back. I was wrong; I didn't mean any of this.' He apologized to beat hell." Reg stayed, and the hijinks continued.

Along with his boisterous personality, Heaton was renowned for riding his buffalo, Grunter, into the rodeo arenas. After entering the arena, Heaton and Grunter would race around and jump into the back of a pick-up truck. Heaton would roll on his shoulders, over the roof, and onto the truck's hood. It was Reg's job to saddle Grunter for Heaton. "Grunter hated Heaton. We'd try to get that goddam buffalo saddled before Heaton would come around, because as soon as Grunter saw Heaton, that buffalo would get rough. We'd saddle Grunter in a rodeo chute, but it was still worth your bloody life if you weren't careful. Of course, Heaton figured out what we were doing, so he'd have to come over and juice Grunter up. He'd go away laughing."

The time came for Grunter to be replaced, so Heaton bought a new buffalo, which he named Coward. Heaton asked Reg to break Coward to ride. As Reg makes very clear, "You break a buffalo with great difficulty. Heaton had a rodeo arena south of Calgary. We put that son of a bitch in the chute, and my friend Ronnie Rolhiser and I took turns getting on this buffalo. We had a saddle on him, and it looked so funny — he looked like a rocking chair. Coward would go out and jump. On the second jump, when his front end hit the ground, he just drove your head into the dirt. There was so much power, he'd blow you out of there. That buffalo bucked us off for two weeks."

Besides Coward, Heaton owned another buffalo named Junior, who clashed constantly with Coward. "While we were breaking Coward, we picketed Junior outside of the corral. One time, instead of bucking, Coward came out of the chute as hard as he could run. He went straight across the arena and just blew the fence away. My friend Ron was on him, and Coward starts fighting with Junior. Junior tears loose from his picket and they're fighting, with Ronnie still on Coward's back."

Reg says he jumped into the pickup truck. "It had stock racks on, which I thought would be good for Ron to jump onto — if I could get it close enough. I chased Ron and the buffalo in the truck. What a mess! Finally, I got close enough for Ron to jump up, but he was so tired he couldn't even see." Eventually, Ron landed safely, and Reg and Ron recaptured Coward and Junior on horseback.

When he wasn't on "buffaloback," Reg was on horseback following chuckwagons. His career outriding behind dirt-spitting wagons began at age fifteen. "You were destined to be an outrider, coming from this family." For years, Reg outrode for his dad's chuckwagon outfit. "Almost exclusively, I specialized in holding the leaders. We did some strange things other people didn't do." For example, Reg grabbed the lead horses earlier than other outriders. Since Ron frequently used new horses, Reg would take hold of the leaders on the racetrack and lead them into the barrel start. Most outriders just grabbed the leaders once they were into the barrels. But Reg ensured the leather tugs were tight. If they were not, they could snap like a Christmas cracker at the starting horn. "As soon as I grabbed the lead team, my focus was on what I was doing."

Reg was primed for every race he outrode. "Whether riding bulls, bucking horses, or driving race cars, you are always wired up and ready to go. Part of that is fear. As an outrider, I hated having a penalty. I suppose all outriders are like that, but to me it seemed I was obsessed with it. I thought that, at the time, I was as good an outrider that there was, if not actually the best. There were probably several other guys who thought they were, too. But it was so important to me not to make a mistake. I probably had a fragile ego. I worked a little harder than some guys — I'd try to nap in the afternoon, and made sure I didn't party too much at night. I tried to make sure I was fresh each night." Reg often rode ten heats each night. But during his career, he feels, there was less pressure placed on outriders, except at Calgary. They raced for fun, not for profit. Today's higher stakes have created greater expectations.

Reg was one of the first outriders to wear a jockey helmet. "Guys always assumed I was afraid I'd break my head, but I kind of have a pointy head, and I could never get a cowboy hat to stay on. I had to pull it right down to my ears; otherwise it'd just pop off. I kept losing my hats. I started wearing a helmet so I wouldn't have to go looking for my damn hat all the time." Reg's helmet saved him a couple of times. During one incident, Reg was riding for Paul Bruderman on a rainy night in Cheyenne. As Reg came around the slippery first turn, his horse's feet went out from under him. As he was pulled down, Reg's head was driven into the ground, pounding his helmet overtop his ears. He shakes his head, remembering: "When we got back to the barn, I discovered the horse had no shoes on. That's why he fell down!"

The second time was in Lethbridge. "Dad rolled his outfit. The wagon came back on its wheels, and Dad was on the ground. Tommy and I were outriding, so we tried to catch the wagon. Tommy was in front of me, so he grabbed the leaders and pulled them towards the fence on the outside rail. Tom caught me between the wagon and the fence. The fence was a chain-link metal fence with the wires pointing straight out of the top. I had to bail over the fence. The wires ripped my arm all to shit, and my head hit one of the posts, splitting the helmet right down — top to bottom. I've still got the scars on my arm from ripping through there."

Following that accident, Reg travelled to Cheyenne with the wagons and rode for Ralph Vigen. Vigen ran a lead horse named Ace Return — a horse some outriders refused to work with. Reg says, "As you held the leaders, Ace Return bit the crap out of your arm. He was a tremendous horse, but a little hard on my arm. I wore great big bandages for protection."

Sometimes the equipment was responsible for Reg's racing thrills. He relates, "I was on the best horse I ever rode, Snappy Joe. I went around the top barrel, and his bridle fell right out. It was gone. Snappy Joe followed the wagon out, and he was really fast — a sprinter; he went right to the front. I was riding beside Dad, sitting there with no bridle, holding nothing, wondering what the hell I was going to do next. I hoped the horse didn't stumble or get me into some kind of switch. My Uncle Jim rode up beside me and said, 'Are you all right?' I said, 'Oh yeah, fine!' He said, 'Well, what can I do?' I said, 'Just run along beside me until we get past the wire.'" As they crossed the finish line, Jim grabbed the horse's foretop and Reg put a finger into the horse's mouth to pull him up. "Good thing Snappy Joe was a sprinter — he got tired quick. That was pretty exciting."

Ron and Iris expected fortitude in the chuckwagon business. Whether you were a friend, a hired man, or a member of the family, you were expected to finish your job. Illnesses and injuries were mere inconveniences. If you could hobble, you could race. A crippled horse received more compassion.

"We put on an exhibition of wagon races for some French pheasant hunters in Lethbridge," Reg relates. At the time, Reg had broken a leg bull riding and was sporting a cast from thigh to toes. "My bull-riding career was short," he laughs. "I got on. I broke my leg in the chute. I got back off. That was it."

While they were in the Lethbridge barns, Iris came up to Reg and said, "You've got to outride."

"I said, 'Sure, right,'" Reg recalls. "My leg was sticking straight out to the side. But Mom said, 'We've got nobody else.' I said, 'How do you expect me to ride?' I didn't have a walking cast and was on crutches.

"Mom brings a horse out and says, 'See if you can swing on.' I could swing on, as long as the horse didn't move around too much. I ended up outriding and throwing stove [instead of holding the leaders]. It was the only place I could easily get up on my horse. The only thing with throwing stove was, if I didn't get the hell out of there, I'd get run over as my wagon made its barrel turn. It worked out. I got on, with one leg in the stirrup and the other leg sticking way out. I got around, and I did two heats for two days." Reg laughs. "I couldn't believe it. Nobody else's mother in the world would ever put them in that situation."

Iris states simply, "I knew he was tough."

For a man of Reg's physical stamina, riding with a broken leg was effortless compared to racing with a heavy heart. But Reg was not just physically tough. "The hardest thing, and the scaredest I've been in my whole life, was the next day after Rod was killed. We went back out and raced that night. 'Course, we had no sleep the night before. We were very emotionally wrecked, and it took the whole day to get your head together to even think about racing.

"The next night, we got there and they did the Cowboy's Prayer, and of course that wrecked you all over again. That was by far the hardest thing I have ever done, to go back and ride that night. I don't think I could do it again, and I don't think I'd try. It was unbelievably tough. I had no focus whatsoever, and my mind was all over the place. To outride that week, under the circumstances, was pretty tough stuff for me. I didn't care if I was ever out there again."

Several nights after Rod was killed, Reg had his own scare on the Stampede track. "I used to tie the racing lines on my outriding horse so there was a loop in them, over the saddle horn. I'd tie them long on the inside, so when I swung on at the top barrel I could just drop my hand down [on the rein] and I'd have instant contact with the horse's mouth [through the bit]."

Reg was riding for driver Bill Greenwood. He says, "Someone had used my bridle that morning. They tried to retie it the same way, but they got it too short on the inside." When the klaxon sounded, Reg and his horse ran to the top barrel. He pulled his horse's lead line towards him, where the larger loop was in the lines. The horse dropped his head down and its head became caught in the line — the rein was across the horse's nose. "I jumped on him and tried to make the bottom barrel. But the more I pulled on him one way, the more I pulled the other. I was going to the track, wide open, and I was trying to get the horse over." Reg could not understand why the horse fought his control. "The horse went right for the bottom barrel and tried to jump it at the last minute. He tripped himself, and went ass over teakettle into the middle of the track."

Reg froze. "I think we were on Barrel 2, and for some reason I was absolutely positive there was another wagon coming. I was lying right in the middle of the track. I can remember that like it was yesterday. I didn't know which way to roll. I just lay there, and then was just amazed that another wagon didn't come . . . they were all gone." He stood up and walked off the track.

By staying motionless, Reg had done the safest thing in the circumstances. Iris explains: "If a rider falls, they are supposed to lay still. Don't move. Don't get up. The horses will miss you if they can."

Things had changed for Reg after the '71 Stampede. "When Rod got killed, all the fun of chuckwagon racing went out of it for me. Before that, it was exciting — jumping through the holes, taking the chances, cutting close. It was all wild and fun. But after Rod got killed, none of it was any fun. It was just work."

In spite of his misgivings, Reg continued to outride for family and friends. He, too, carried on. But, while racing at Calgary in the late 1970s, he was seriously injured outriding. The accident solidified his decision to retire.

Recalling the race, Reg says, "Driver Dave Lewis missed a line coming round the top barrel [Lewis was driving the outfit to the left of Reg]." In missing the line, Lewis's horses swept wide around their top barrel. When they finally turned, they ran into the unsuspecting Reg, knocking him down between his own barrels. Reg was propelled into the path of his own chuckwagon. "My own outfit lined out over top of me. The wagon's wheel hit my leg, bounced, and hit my chest. It caved my chest all in. It broke my ribs, punctured my lung, and then came over my head." He recalls, "Mom was doing the radio at the top of the grandstand. After I got run over, the first thing I practically remember is Mom standing there. I thought she must have flown down from the top of the grandstand."

At the hospital the next day, Reg complained about a sore head. "The stupid doctor came out of the room with a bolt, gave it to Mom, and said, 'I took this out of your son's head.'" Somehow a bolt from the wagon's doubletree had embedded itself in Reg's skull.

Unlike those from his previous mishaps, Reg's injuries produced unrelenting pain. "Two weeks before my accident, I had been working the starting gates at the racetrack. It is a boring job. You load the horses, which only takes a minute, and then you wait a half-hour for the next race." To fill in time, Reg did chin-ups and push-ups on the steel bars. "I don't know if that added to it — working the muscles out for a couple of weeks and then being locked right down — but it took about three months to really stop hurting. Prior to this accident, I'd had three broken legs, three or four broken arms, broken ribs, and all kinds of stuff. You hurt for a couple of days, but then it's an ache for another couple of weeks." Reg laughs. "But this hurt for a long time. That's way too long to hurt!"

It was the last race Reg outrode until his brother called him out of retirement. In 1980 Tom needed Reg for the Battle of the Giants in High River. "I was in Edmonton with the racehorses, and a bunch of kids got hurt in a big wreck. Tommy phoned us to ride, since they were short of outriders. Jim [his uncle], Gary and Doug Lauder [his cousins], and I rode for Tom. It was a whole-family win." It was the last outriding buckle Reg won.

Following his outriding injury, Reg focused completely on his flourishing career training thoroughbred racehorses. "It wasn't that I got hurt that I quit outriding, but I was already at the track and had quite a few horses. I didn't want to leave the horses with somebody else. I didn't have time to both outride and train."

Ron became a trainer almost by accident. "I used to run bush races with Mom. One year, we thought our horses were good enough to go to the A tracks. Mom was going to take them, and I went in with her. We went to get Mom's trainer's license, and they asked, 'Are you going to be here all the time?' Mom said, 'No, I'm going to be with the wagons when they're on.' The track stewards said, 'Who's going to be here?' And Mom said, 'Well, Reg, I guess.' They said, 'Well, maybe Reg better have the license.' So I got the trainer's license. Mom went back to the farm, and I never left the track for twenty years."

Before he named his stables, Reg set up a numbered company. But, he says, "Just to have a number didn't seem right. I asked Mom, 'Do you want to put a name on it? What name do you want?' Mom said, 'What do you think?' I came up with the answer right then." Checker Board Stables was christened, and Reg chose the family's colors. Any jockey seen wearing black-and-white checkered silks was riding a horse for Reg Glass.

When Reg began training, betting on horse races was the only legal means to gamble. As a licensed trainer, Reg took responsibility for ensuring his horses met the regulations, including those on the use of painkillers and correct weights on the horses. He also claimed horses and bought new horses at yearling sales, and then conditioned them to race. He picked the rider, picked the races, and chose the gallop boy.

When he entered the racehorse business, Reg says, "I was just a cowboy kid with an ego, who didn't want to let everybody know how stupid I was. I didn't know how far to gallop a horse or how fast to work a horse. I went in, hid, and watched. In those days, the coffee shop was where everyone spent tons of time. The old trainers would sit in there BS-ing, and I'd sneak in and sit down beside them. If I was wondering about something, I'd sneak it into the conversation and let three or four of the old boys figure out the pros and cons about the problem. I'd sit there and soak it all up. I'd try and direct conversation to learn as much as I could."

Since Reg came from a chuckwagon family, his training perspective was unique. "The racetrack has its own schedules and its own way of doing things. When I went in there, I knew absolutely nothing about any of that. Our family did everything different." Reg broke all his racehorses to drive hooked to a cart or a wagon. "Thoroughbreds are very finely made athletes, and they're very susceptible to leg injuries. The more time you give them to get everything tightened back down again, the more you can keep the weight off them, the better. I figured it was quite an edge to train the first month or six weeks by driving without the weight of a rider."

From their feed to their exercise, Reg calculated a common sense formula to win. He trained his horses sympathetically. "If I wouldn't like it, why would the horses?" Generally, six to eighteen horses were in Reg's Checker Board Stables. "I was always trying to make my horses happy. I'd get my horses out of their stalls, or I'd put the horses in the sunshine. It's a long haul being in the stall basically twenty-three hours a day. I'd hand-walk them rather than hot-walk them [using a machine]. I tried to take advantage of being a smaller barn by doing more for the horses. The guys with forty horses couldn't do that."

Reg retired from training in the 1990s, when video lottery terminals and other new forms of legalized gambling depleted the money being invested in horses. Summing up his career, he reflects, "It was very interesting work — a tremendously mental thing. I was always looking for every inch to improve things, because in flat races the times are even tighter than wagon racing. By gaining half a second, it could move your horse up three or four classes. After all it took to train a horse and win a race, you felt you'd really achieved something."

From thoroughbreds to buffalos to broncos, Reg has lived a rowdy and rugged life. This cowboy learned to manage and redirect his pain, building up internal calluses that reflect the durability bred into and reinforced by his family. He explains, "Say, if you break your arm or your leg. You go to the hospital, get a cast on it, and take a couple of painkillers. For a couple of days it hurts quite a bit, but then it's just an ache. Once you've done that, been through it and handled it, I think it lessens your fear of something like that happening again. It's not fun, but it's nothing to be afraid of, either. Once you've been hurt a few times, you learn you can handle your hurt. I think you do learn how to mentally remove yourself from the pain."

Reg's pain management is not a widely cultivated skill. "My doctor thinks I'm absolutely nuts. He can't believe anybody would put themselves into a position to be hurt. He loves to ask, 'Where'd that come from? What's this scar from?'" He adds, "I had one session where I was in for three or four different things within a pretty short period. The doctor said, 'I wish I had another half-dozen guys like you. That's all I'd have to look after.'"

Throughout his life, Reg has concentrated on the task at hand. He shares the family's ability not to question or calculate the potential for calamity. Reg simply performs. "You still get scared of doing something dangerous. You'd have to be stupid not to be scared. But you just learn to focus on what you have to do not to get hurt. You concentrate on doing it properly, rather than concentrating on what could happen or how you could get hurt." Exemplifying the Glass vigor, Reg states, "You kind of get a fearless attitude."

8

The Homestretch Flier

I always used to tell myself, "I'm going to sit down and just throw the lines at them." But even after thirty years, once my horses started to make a move, I always got off the seat and threw the lines. I never did quit doing it, and my son Jason does it too.
— TOM GLASS

"I get a little envious of Tom," says Reg Glass of his younger brother. "He always seems to be the luckiest guy in the world. Whatever he does turns out good." He laughs. "I don't know how much is talent and how much is luck."

Tom Glass followed his older brother onto the racetrack. At age ten, he began jockeying his parent's racehorses, and he rode till he was fourteen. By then he was too large to jockey, but brawny enough to outride. Tom recalls his first outriding race: "On the way back from Cheyenne, our family stopped to race at Casper, Wyoming. Hank Willard, a very good friend of my dad's, asked me to outride." He smiles. "I had a hell of a time. Halfway around the track I was still trying to get on my horse."

The next year, at age fifteen, Tom asked his dad if he could outride for him. "Dad said, 'No, go practice for somebody else first.'" So he did. Bill Greenwood offered Tom a job, and, as part of Greenwood's outfit, Tom won the Calgary Stampede. He says, "My dad hired me after that."

Two more years passed before Tom tried driving a chuckwagon competitively. He recalls, "When I was seventeen, I went to Texas with my friend Doyle Mullaney. I just went along for the ride, but Cliff Claggett got me driving a pony chuckwagon outfit in Mission, Texas. That's when the bug bit. I just loved it. We threw everything together with those pony wagons, and of course we tried to put a show on. It was kind of wild.

"I came back and slapped together an outfit. I bought three old horses and borrowed a grey horse from some Gleichen Indian boys." In 1966, using four of Lloyd Nelson's outriding horses, Tom ran his first outfit in Calgary.

Tom was comfortable in a chuckwagon. Before his first Stampede race, he had ridden hundreds of miles in a wagon with his father. Tom developed his driving style by observation. "Dad never said too much about driving. I probably learned more about the horse side [of operations] from Dad rather than the driving part of it. The driving you just had to do. You spend so much time in the wagon together, watching the other person and how he drives. You try different things. I tried holding the lines a little differently; I tried sitting down. But I didn't like either one of them. So I stood back up and held the lines just like my dad did."

Few drivers employ Ron Glass's unusual style of grip. Tom, his son Jason, Richard Cosgrave, and Colt Cosgrave have numbered among the few. Tom explains the technique: "Most guys drive with what they call a full hand. The drivers put the reins underneath their bottom finger — the little finger — and over between their thumb and first finger, so it's a full-fisted drive. In comparison, Dad, myself, and Jason drive through our fingers — we have the first finger between the two lines. Lots of guys have tried it and said they're not strong enough to drive that way. It's more comfortable to me, because I can change my lines easier, and we change our lines a lot. It's not as strong a way to drive, but I always liked it, because, if a horse stumbles, I can pick up my lines quicker. I can open my fingers and let them slide, rather than pulling the lines out of my hand."

Tom's fingers were gifted not only in handling wagon lines, but also around a barber's chair. Tom left high school to learn the barbering trade from Pete Mullaney in Regina. Then he and fellow driver Dallas Dorchester both worked as barbers in Calgary. After a short career in hair-styling, Tom worked in construction, framing houses during the winter months. During his early years of driving, Tom also continued outriding to cover expenses. "I outrode four heats so I could get enough money to pay my outriders. [The money from] the extra outriding heats is what I bought horses with."

Tom's commitment to wagon racing intensified after an injury to his father. "Dad fell on his elbow and hurt a nerve. His hand did not work very well. He did not have much strength; his hand was always cold." Eventually, Ron wore a glove on his injured hand during most of the summer. "It got to where he could hardly hang on to the lines. In Stettler, Tom Dorchester was teasing Dad and said, 'Why don't you let the kid drive?'"

Ron said, "Okay." Using his dad's outfit, Tom recounts, "I got flukey and won second-day money." The next week, in Ponoka, he again used Ron's horses, and at age twenty Tom won his first show. "Dad kind of quit after that show. We did race together a couple of times. When we did, he could always outrun me."

Tom's racing ambitions were also galvanized by a young "King." "Kelly Sutherland probably has as much to do with me getting serious about wagon racing as anybody. Kelly was a hotshot kid, and he showed the rest of us young guys that we could beat Dad, Bill Greenwood, Hally Walgenbach, and the other old boys that were hard to beat. Kelly was the first young guy to do it. Kelly of course had a good outfit, but he was also cocky. He kind of came swaggering around. Kelly was kicking everybody's butt, and I thought maybe I should get more serious and take a run at him. I thought maybe I could beat the old boys, too. Pretty soon we were all running near the top."

Tom's career lasted from 1966 to 1999. He calls himself fortunate, because, throughout that career, he endured only a few serious wrecks. The first one occurred at home. "I was in the field with my dad. We were turning the barrels and the wagon went up on two wheels. I thought it was coming back down again, so I climbed up to the high side and hung on to the hoops. It went over, and it must have thrown me twenty feet. I landed right on my face.

"I picked myself up, turned around, and my dad is standing there beside the wagon with all four horses. He's got the lines still in his hand, but the wagon is laying on its side." While Tom was flying, Ron had jumped out and stopped the horses.

Ron said, "Come on, kid, get over here."

"While I spit dirt, I got over and helped him push the wagon back up. Dad laughed about that for the rest of the day."

Several years later, Tom duplicated that free flying, but, out of "just stupidity," he broke his ankle. "I set up two steel barrels out in the field," he says. "Of course, you're supposed to be smart enough not to use steel barrels. I ran over a barrel — it got underneath the wagon and lifted it up. Just as it wobbled and was going to tip over, I jumped out. I tried to do the same thing Dad did."

Tom landed heavily on one leg, fell, and could not stand up. "The team came around in a circle. They were going to run over me, so I crawled and crawled. They came by and missed me. I kept trying to get up, but I couldn't get up. I didn't realize my ankle was broken. With the circulation cut off, it felt like the lines were wrapped around my ankle. I looked down — the sole of my boot was lying to the side of my leg. I thought my boot had fallen off . . . but my foot was still in it! It had just snapped right around in a circle."

With his leg in a cast, Tom was unable to drive. For two months, Eddie Wiesner drove his horses and ran over three barrels during competitions. "He did not get along too well with my outfit." Tom was impatient to return to driving. "I modified my seat — took the springs off and nailed it to the side of the box. I slid the seat up about six inches from the front, so I could jam myself in there with a cast on my foot. If that wagon had ever tipped over, I don't know how I would've got away from it, but you don't think of them things when you're nineteen years old."

It was not the last time a wagon spit Tom out. Racing in High River, he explains, "Reg was holding my leaders. His horse laid into my lead team at the top barrel, and his stirrup got caught on my left lead horse's harness, on a bellyband. Reg was just getting on his horse, and when my outfit went back to the track they took his horse with them. Reg was just flung through the air. I remember seeing him skidding across the arena, and I wondered, 'What in the hell is going on?' I went to go to the track and I've got *three* leaders — my lead team plus his outriding horse tied on! Of course, I can't steer the outriding horse, so he ducked up the track and ran over the bottom barrel. The barrel went underneath the wagon and upset me — threw me out. I went across the track."

As the wagon went over, Tom says, "I jumped and landed on my feet. I thought, 'This is pretty good,' except my body was doing forty miles per hour and my feet were only doing ten. I purdy near made it all the way across the track, but then the momentum piled me up into the fence. Away the horses went, ripping the box off of the wagon. The horses were all fine. And after the guys flipped the wagon back on its wheels, I actually drove it back around. But I did have to build a new wagon."

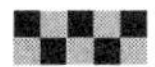

Throughout Tom's storied career, his outfit was renowned for its breakneck homestretch charges. He continually won races by coming from behind. His voice roaring, his body surging, and the lines pumping, Tom electrified the crowd. He could lift twenty thousand people out of their seats. Wagon fans were in for some excitement when Tom Glass was in a race.

Tom's homestretch drives were calculated. To save his horses, he rested them on the backstretch, hauling on their lines, letting them catch their breath. "You've got the wraps on them pretty good. You're pulling on them, and they want to go." At the third corner, he would turn them loose. "By that time, you've been pulling on them long enough.

"I got in some wicked holes, because I always came from behind. I had so much run that I used to get jammed in there, but I always seemed to find a way through. If a guy gave me room enough to get one horse in there, my old horse Carrufer would make a hole. I could pull on him, but he had a terribly hard mouth. As soon as that hole opened, old Carrufer would bail in there. He'd make room."

To foil Tom's charges, his competitors used blocking techniques. "As I came by, guys would start fading out, or they would block me in a little bit. But we always used to do it to each other. If I knew a guy was coming from behind, the old saying was, 'Go around.' You never let any wagon, or an outrider riding for another wagon, come through on the inside near the rail."

Today, drivers are no longer permitted to "wagoncheck" their competitors. "You used to be able to drive like that [coming from behind through a hole], but at Calgary you can't do that anymore. Now you have to pick a lane, do your thing, and let the guy next to you have a run." The race rules were changed to make the final stretch safer for horses. In Tom's era, when the wagons dashed through small holes, wooden wheels would collide and get smashed. "It used to be quite a bit wilder. I've seen the spokes fly. Kelly and I used to rub each other, and the wood would be flying in the air, usually from the front wheels. It was part of wagon racing. As long as it was wagon to wagon, it was let go. Now they give penalties for it."

Tom's reputation for full-bore, head-on charges to the finish proved problematic in 1988. Yards from the finish line, his lead horse fell. To twenty thousand Stampede fans, he seemed to be forcing his injured horse across the finish line. The accident threw his passion for wagon racing into a stew of public controversy.

The accident occurred on the second-last night of racing. He was leading the Rangeland Derby by nearly eight seconds and, if he remained in the top four, he would race in the Stampede final. That fateful evening, Tom says, "I used my horses Mike and Dale, Carrufer and Snapper.

Snapper was probably the best left-hand leader I ever had." As he was galloping down the homestretch, Snapper's leg broke. "He fell down, but we were going wide open, so he was dragged for a hundred yards before the horses stopped. The SPCA said, 'Glass drove his horse across the finish line!'" Critics claimed Tom had pushed his horses so he could make the Stampede final. But, Tom argues, "You don't say *Whoa!* to the other three horses and just put the brake on like a car. Just the momentum kept us going. My outriders couldn't even stop fast enough to stay with the wagon. All four outriders went by me, passed me, and went across the finish line." He adds, "I received eight seconds in penalties, putting me even with the rest of the guys.

"That was probably the worst horse accident for me. Snapper was one of the family — he was my mom's favorite. It is terrible to lose a horse. If a horse is older and has had a good life, it's not as bad. Maybe I sound sadistic or whatever, but a young, strong horse that gets hurt — it's a shitty deal. I've been fortunate; I haven't lost a lot of horses wagon racing. But it is part of the game."

The Glasses were in the media spotlight. The press vilified Tom for urging his horses on, and the Glasses had to fight the media's misrepresentation of wagon racing. When reporters do not understand the cowboys' commitment to their horses, they often distort the stories. "I hated them guys [reporters with cameras]. If there ever was a wreck with a horse, they'd run over there. They don't try to be good about it; they just take a picture of the horse's broken leg. The next day in the paper, there it is.

"Once we had a wreck in Cloverdale. A bridle fell off a horse and the outfit ran away on me. We went three laps around the track, because, without a bridle, I couldn't stop them. So, at the end, the horses finally piled up. They weren't hurt, but one horse was laying down underneath on the ground. A reporter was taking pictures of the horses and saying, 'Look at that, you killed that horse! They should shoot them drivers instead of shooting horses. You killed the horse!' I was so frustrated and so angry, because the horse is laying down there, and my arms were like rubber [from] trying to stop them." The reporter kept coming closer. "It was just way too tempting. I stood on my wagon box, stepped over onto the rail — his camera was just a perfect distance, and I kicked it over his head. The camera flipped in the air and landed on the ground. He didn't have a camera anymore. But he still ran about fifty yards away, stood there, and kept yapping till somebody else took him away."

When not punting cameras, Tom was devising strategies to surpass his friends. Chuckwagon racing revolves around a social rivalry. "The whole thing about wagon racing is you're trying to outrun your friends. It's about competition. Richard Cosgrave and I used to let each other through [on the inside] once in a while, but not any other guy. Richard would give you three feet going around a corner. Kelly Sutherland would give you three inches. And I was the same — I was an aggressive driver. If you were on the inside of me, you'd better be within six inches of the rail, because I wasn't going to let you run two feet off there. That's the way Kelly drives, and Dallas Dorchester, too. We pushed each other."

The cowboys' competition extended past the track gate. "Dallas Dorchester did what he had to do to win. He's a good friend of mine, but he might talk to one of my outriders, asking them to go ride for him. He wanted to win. You're the best friends at the barn, but not necessarily on the track."

Since the first evening that Tom and Kelly Sutherland hooked up, the "King" has been the driver to beat. As two of the best drivers of their generation, Tom and Kelly shared many thrilling head-to-head races. Tom says, "I wanted to outrun Kelly. He's fun to outrun." He laughs. "I think everybody likes to beat Kelly, because they like to outrun the guy that's on top, especially if they're a little cocky about it. I have no problem saying that. Kelly knows he's cocky, and he likes that aspect of it. But Kelly can drive a wagon. He gets the job done, one way or another. One thing I always remember about Kelly is when he introduced all the wagon drivers in Grande Prairie in '83 or '84. I had an awesome outfit, and Kelly said, 'Here's Tom Glass. This is probably the hardest man there is to outrun in the wagon business.' That was a great compliment." For thirty years, Tom and Kelly were often closely matched in the final heat. For example, in the 1987 Calgary Stampede final, Kelly beat Tom to the wire, but one of Kelly's outriders had knocked over a barrel, and Tom claimed his second Stampede trophy.

Despite all the exhilarating, challenging, and impassioned races Kelly and Tom shared, one race was simply annoying. "My most frustrating race was in Strathmore in 1994, the year Ward Willard won the World championship." He recalls the championship heat: "Kelly, Ward, and I were in the final. My outfit was running hard, really smoking on the outside. Kelly and I turned side by side, and he had me by half a horse-length. But I was staying with him, head to head, all the way round the third corner. He knew it and I knew it that, when we headed home, I was going to get him. Once we straightened out, I should have the horsepower to outrun him.

"But Kelly worried about me too much. As he pushed me out on the corner, trying to make me go around farther, he opened a hole in along the rail. There was no hole there really; it was tight — it was only three feet wide — but Ward drove his outfit in there. I don't know how he got through there without piling up, but they made it through the hole. Ward went down the rail. I think he outran me by 3/100 of a second. Kelly was in the middle, and he was 6/100 behind me. It cost me the World [championship]. If I had had another horse-length [ahead of Kelly], Ward would have never got through the rail, because that's where Kelly would've been. Kelly would have been tight on the rail, so nobody could come on the inside."

Coming off the track, Tom hollered at Kelly, "What the hell are you doing?" Kelly just shrugged. "He knew he screwed up as soon as Ward went through there. I can't say I wouldn't have done the same thing, because he knew I had him on the outside. He was more worried about me than Ward. I think it was a shock to him to all of a sudden see Ward." Despite losing, Tom appreciates Kelly's competitive strategy. "I think that's the way you should drive a wagon, especially if you're 'wagon on wagon.'

I don't like playing with somebody's horses, but if you're head and head, and if you're on the rail, get on the rail. I think the guys are a little gentler now, which is good. They don't push as hard as we used to."

For Tom, every chuckwagon race was exhilarating. Each race had separate nuances. Each race had a special strategy. Each race was a rush. And yet, among his thousands of laps around the track, one race stands out.

The Glasses owned a horse named Swing Leader. "I hooked our horse Swing Leader only twice on the breaking cart. The third time I hooked him, I put him up on the right-hand lead. He stayed in that position the rest of his life. He was the most natural leader you've ever seen — just amazing. He turned the top barrel with his eyeball on it, just like a barrel-racing horse. I had to have a big wheel team behind him, because he was turning in a hurry."

Tom recounts the last race Swing Leader ran in Cheyenne, Wyoming. "We drew the barrels [for the final heat], and I wanted any barrel but Barrel 1. So of course I drew Barrel 1." By that last night, Tom's aggregate time lead was so large that, even if he hit both barrels, he could still win the show. "The only way I couldn't win was if I upset. And I *could* upset on Barrel 1. Barrel 1 is a really a hard barrel in Cheyenne — it's long, and really hard to turn. It's set really tough. I thought, if this team works like it's been working all week, there's no way I'm going to make that bottom barrel. I'll be going way too fast."

Despite drawing Barrel 1, Tom used his potent team, which included Swing Leader. "The horses started so hard they literally nearly knocked me off the seat. When we turned the top barrel, I figured there was no way I was going to make the bottom barrel. But we turned the bottom, and I was on two wheels — I was half tipped over. That team just kept running so hard to the first corner."

Tom was racing on two wheels. "No exaggeration — my wagon was balanced for probably one hundred yards, deciding whether it was going to go over or back. I just kept pumping on that left wheeler to pull it down. Finally, it came back. It slapped back on the ground, back on its wheels." That night, Tom's outfit broke the track record. "Those horses were just phenomenal. It was probably the most exciting race of my career." At the end of Cheyenne's nine days, Tom and his horses had won the Frontier Days championship by twenty-five seconds.

Throughout his championship races, Tom Glass experienced both adrenaline and doubt. "I've sat in the wagon and thought, 'Why the hell do you do this? Do you really need this?' You're half scared and half nervous, but if you're not half scared and half nervous you shouldn't be there. You need to be keyed up; that way you can react. When you're wound up and the horn goes, then you know what it's all about."

In his career's last fifteen years, Tom raced in the Calgary Stampede final eleven times. "The adrenaline for the $50,000 is amazing. When you pull into the last race, it's *the Calgary Stampede.* I don't even know whether it was the money, but you've made it into the best four." In the bulk of Stampede wagon races, Tom says, "Usually, you don't even hear the crowd. The odd time when I made the big run — smoking, coming down the homestretch — I could hear the crowd." But, he adds, "In the final, you do."

In his first Stampede final, Tom recalls, "The crowd was so loud you couldn't hear. You tried to listen for the horn, but the crowd was just screaming. My old legs were just a-knockin' — banging the front of the box, wanting to go. It's an amazing rush." When Tom raced in the 1983 final, he never did hear the horn. "The horses heard it. I never hollered or did anything, but the horses were going. I was halfway to the top barrel and thought, 'God, I hope the horn went.' I knew that it did, because everybody was moving with me."

Tom and the cowboys voiced their concerns about the noise. Today, the Stampede audience is asked to be quiet before the final race so the cowboys can hear the klaxon. But as soon as the klaxon sounds, the crowd erupts with unbridled cheering for the cowboys.

There was satisfaction for Tom in every loud victory. And whether he was racing in honor of an injured friend or using special horses, there was a distinctive element to each championship. One such Stampede victory occurred in 1992. "[That Stampede] it rained so much. We ran in a foot of mud the whole ten days. It was just slop. It wasn't heavy or hard going, but the water just laid on the track. And yet my outfit just loved it. They were way better horses in the mud than on a dry track."

In the drawing for barrel positions, Tom pulled the formidable Barrel 4. Up to 1992, only one driver had won the Stampede off Barrel 4. "It is such a letdown when you're up on stage and draw Barrel 4. You think, 'Aw shit, that's it. Who can win the $50,000 off 4? It's such a letdown. You think you're just out there for the ride." But regardless of the barrel draw, Tom emphasizes, "You go for it."

"My outfit just cracked off the barrels," he recalls, "and I went to the engine on the inside. I hung in there on the outside all the way around, and won it." In classic Glass style, Tom had surged down the homestretch to inch past George Normand's outfit. He did not realize that Normand had knocked over a barrel. "I thought I had to beat him at the wire, and [the winning margin] couldn't have been much more than a foot."

Tom credits his sustained success in wagon racing to his supportive family, as well as to his horses. "You're not successful in the wagon business without family around you. You can see all the guys who have done well, and they've got a lot of help from their families. My daughter, Kristy, and everybody chipped in. When the race was over in Calgary, we had eight head of horses coming back there at one time. Nobody can look after that many, and they all need attention *right now*. They all need to be walked, cooled, brushed. And you've got to make sure they don't get too much water [a horse may develop colic if it drinks too much too quickly].

"The women will tell you that a wagon driver can't succeed without the girls in the barn, and they're probably right. They do a lot of work and offer a lot of moral support. They put up with you when you're pissed off and you don't win. If I had a bad run, they knew enough to leave me alone for half an hour. I'd always shake it off, but I'd pout first."

Part of Tom's frustration stems from his competitive, ambitious nature. "I liked to win. If you like to win anything, you'll be competitive. I don't think I lived by this philosophy, but my friend Brent Woolsey said, 'Show me a good loser, and I'll show you a loser.' I don't believe in that strongly, but it's part of it. It's got to bother you. If you're competitive and it doesn't bother you to lose, you won't win much."

Tom demonstrated his tenacious competitive valor on the Ponoka racetrack. But he wasn't driving or even in the wagon. "That year I had two wagon outfits. It was the last day of Ponoka, and Doug Lauder, my cousin, was driving my second outfit." Tom's two best wheel horses, Dale and Mike, were on Lauder's outfit.

"Doug came around after the race, pulling and pulling on the horses, but he couldn't stop them." Doug had a runaway and it was three days before the Calgary Stampede. "I was standing there watching the race, and I'm thinking, 'There's my good outfit. I'm going to Calgary in two days, and they're going to make three laps of the track!' I had visions of my horses being played out for the week in Calgary. I was just having a fit."

Tom acted instinctively. "I ran over and grabbed one of my outriding horses, a little mare who I knew could fly. I jumped on her." But as Tom leapt on the mare, one of her stirrups broke, so he had no means to lift up and pull on the runaway horses' harness. "I got out ahead of Doug. I was going to try and grab one of the horses, but I knew I couldn't stop them off the mare without any leverage." He had one option — to get into the chuckwagon. "As the outfit came by on the backstretch, I got up on one knee, stood up on the horse a little bit, and jumped in the wagon. I took all the hide off of my belly from going over, and hit my head on the side of the box." Tom crawled up to Doug, grabbed the lines, and slowed the team. "It was pretty wild. I got over to the barns and a committee guy from Ponoka came up and said, 'Jesus! Glass, we'd pay a lot of money if you'd do that tomorrow night in front of the grandstand.'"

He laughs. "That's the wildest stunt I've done, and it was in a wagon race." Tom always did what he had to do to win. His desire propelled his nerve, and his daring ambition made him a dashing champion.

9

Never Forgotten

When Tom and Richard were racing in the same heat, the question we were asked most often was "Who do you cheer for?" I said, "I cheer for both of them, but I spend Richard's money."
— TARA GLASS

Like her brothers, Tara Glass grew up in trailers and barns. "We were all involved with the horses all the time. We looked after the outriding horses, fed them, and cleaned the barn." The horses, the lifestyle, and the wagon men would leave an indelible impression on her life.

Every summer, Tara was ready to reunite with the wagon community. "We'd leave in May and go to the end of August. We'd live with those people four months of the year. It's pretty close, very tight. You might be mad with someone after the end of a race, but you've got to get over it, because you travel with them all summer. There is a lot of 'forgive and forget' as you go down the road. Everybody kind of knew everybody."

Tara met her first husband, outrider and driver Eddie Wiesner, through the wagons. Wiesner joined the extended wagon family as a teenager, working as a hired man for the Cosgrave family. Tara and Eddie were married in 1969, and their daughter, Kim, was born in 1970.

Wiesner proved he could fit into the Glass family while training horses with Tom. Tom was driving a green horse, and Eddie was standing behind him in the wagon. In place of barrels, they had set up two five-gallon pails full of rocks. Tom recalls, "I turned the top barrel. As I came to the bottom, I leaned forward to give this green horse a little extra line, and of course I hit the bucket with my wheel. It threw me out of the wagon." Tom hit the ground, taking the four lines with him. "The horses jerked the lines out of my hand, and away the outfit went down the field. Eddie was behind the seat riding with me, and now the lines are on the ground. He's standing there with four horses running as hard as they can, with no control.

"You had to know Eddie Wiesner. It was like watching a movie. Eddie climbs over the seat and then climbs over the front of the box. He reaches up on the horses' backs, grabs the lines, and climbs back in. This all happens within half a mile. At the end of that half-mile there was a barbed-wire fence and a ditch — there was a big wreck coming! Just before they get to the fence, Eddie turns them around in a circle and drives back down. He drives up to me, smiles, and says, 'Next time you do that, I'm jumping out beside you.'"

Tom recalls, "I wasn't too worried about Eddie — I knew he'd look after himself — but I was worried about the horses. You're scared for your horses. With no control, the barbed-wire fence would've cut them all up. I was just hoping Eddie could get up there and do something."

Tara and Eddie separated after nine years. In 1978, Tara married wagon driver Richard Cosgrave. "Richard and I grew up together, and we were really good friends for years. We were both living in Okotoks, and started going out." Richard was six years younger and, like Tara, the third generation of a prominent chuckwagon family. His father, Bob, had won the

Calgary Stampede twice, and his grandfather, Dick, had won the Stampede a record ten times.

At the end of their first year of marriage, Richard bought a herd of breeding cows and took responsibility for his family's farm near Hand Hills, Alberta. When they left Okotoks, Tara recalls, "We left the mountains, and it was hard to get used to. All my family was still in High River." Tara was twenty-nine years old, their first son, Colt, was just a baby, and she was pregnant with their second son, Chad.

Tara and Richard were supportive partners. While he was racing, "Richard never went to a show that I didn't go to," Tara says. "Even one time when he was sick, a hired man and I took Richard's outfit to Grande Prairie and we found a driver up there. We looked after the horses, and Norm Cuthbertson and Reg Johnstone drove the wagon.

"Richard was a Hand Hills rancher," Tara says of her husband. "He didn't really seek the limelight. He was comfortable in the barn. He loved to visit with people. He was quiet and very easygoing, a lot like our son Colt." Despite the Cosgrave reputation, Richard never considered himself a celebrity. "When people came and asked for our autographs, we kind of laughed. Richard loved to visit, talk to kids, but in his own element. He didn't like to go to fancy things or go to the midway to sign autographs for people he didn't know. That's the way Richard always was — put him in the barn. He was a very gentle, loveable kind of person. He would help the new guys, lend them a horse, or show them anything he could to help them to get better. And he was the same at home — he was everybody's neighbor. Everybody liked him."

Richard Cosgrave died on August 7, 1993, from injuries suffered in a wagon race at Kamloops, British Columbia. It was the final day of the '93 chuckwagon season. Tara says, "When you look back, it's all probably total coincidence, but [1993] was the best year he had. His outfit was really working, he had good horses, and we'd just bought a hundred head of heifers that spring. Then, in July, he won the truck in Calgary [for the Stampede's lowest aggregate time]. Everything seemed to be picture-perfect at the time."

Tara recalls nothing unusual about the day Richard was hurt. "We were in Kamloops, and Richard hated the heat. He spent the afternoon watching TV in the trailer while all of us went to the beach." The day before the accident, their son, Colt, had broken his collarbone playing football on the beach. "Colt always drove in the wagon with Richard [before the race], but since he was hurt, that night our youngest son, Chad, rode in the wagon. That was the first time he ever got to ride in it."

Remembering that evening, Iris says, "Richard always called me 'Granny.' He came to borrow one of Tom's horses. I asked him, 'What are you doing, mister?' He said, 'Tom said I could borrow this horse. Can I have him, Granny? Is he a good one?' I said, 'Yes, you sure can, and you'll really like him.' Away he went. That was the last time I talked to him."

Recounting Richard's race, Tara says, "It wasn't a big accident or a big wreck. The wheel just snapped off the wagon [after turning the bottom barrel]. Richard looked at it a couple of times, the wagon lost its balance, and he fell out." When he landed on the track, the wagon's back wheel ran over him.

Ironically, Richard's wagon had been reinforced. "Richard had a steel axle put in," Iris Glass explains, "and he thought it would never break. But the wheel broke right off the steel."

Tara remembers sitting on the fence, saying, "Aw, the wheel broke." She reflects: "You think when there is a big wreck, things should happen, but [this accident] wasn't [like that]. His death shouldn't have been the outcome of it."

Tom was sitting with his outfit, waiting for the next race. "They said Richard's wheel fell off and he fell out of the wagon. I never did go down there. If I had had any idea that it was even serious, I would've had somebody else take my horses." He, too, comments, "It was a strange thing — it wasn't a big wreck."

Tara and Iris went to the hospital. When she was sitting there, Tara says, "They kept saying we could go in and see him in a minute. They just kept saying this for three-quarters of an hour to an hour. All the time we felt we were going to be able to go in any minute, we might be there a few days extra, but we'd be going home. Then the doctor came out and told us he wasn't going to make it. We went in — and he was gone.

"I think that was the hardest part — knowing you were there, but you couldn't get in. You didn't get to say goodbye, and we should've, because we were right there. When you do get to say it to someone, you realize how important it is to say goodbye. It means a lot after. Richard's dad, Bob, died in January 2000, and we'd known he was sick. We were with him when he was in the hospital, and you left with a totally different feeling — of being able to say goodbye. But we never dreamt, never dreamt, that it would happen. Even waiting there — you look back, and maybe I should've said, 'I'm going in' — but you never dreamt that would happen."

"Quite a few of us were sitting in the [hospital] waiting room," Iris recalls. "The nurse would come in, saying, 'He's doing fine. Tell Tara he's doing okay.' Then they called a Code Blue. I'll never forget that call of Code Blue. We knew that was [Richard], because they'd rushed him into Emergency, and nobody else had come while we were sitting there. 'Code Blue. Code Blue.'"

Tara feels the hospital staff may have not realized the seriousness of Richard's condition. "They had the x-ray machine right there, and they kept trying to stabilize him. They thought they were getting him okay, but they never could." Afterwards, a nurse told Tara, "Don't ever think he wasn't in the right place or more could've been done somewhere else. This is one of the very best hospitals in B.C." Richard died of internal bleeding. "Richard's left lung had been severed in half," explains Tara. "They initially said his aorta was cut off from his heart, but when they did the autopsy it was his lung."

After leaving the hospital, "I took a taxi to the grounds," Iris recalls, "because I knew Tom was there. Tom was going to come to the hospital once he got the horses put away. I went back and told him. God, the whole place went wild. Those poor kids — Chad was twelve and Colt was fifteen. That was something to tell them. Chad — he cried and cried. Colt wouldn't cry. He's tough, or he pretended he was tough. I got Mitch Sutherland, Kirk Sutherland's kid and Colt's best friend. I said, 'Mitch, come and talk to Colt.' So he came in and took a hold of Colt's hand, and, oh my God, did that kid cry. He just sobbed and sobbed for an hour while Mitch held his hand. Crying is the best thing you could ever do."

When Tom walked into the family's trailer, Iris says, "Chad ran over to him and said, 'Tom, who's going to feed our cows?' That was like Chad — the ranch was everything. That was all he could think of, that he had no dad to feed his cows."

Twenty-two years had passed since Rod Glass was killed, and this loss was no easier. Reflecting on how her family had lost a son and a son-in-law to the sport they cherish, Iris says, "When you're going, you're going because your time is all written down up there. It doesn't matter what you're doing, where you're at, or who you are. That's when you're going to go. They're up there, they're happy, they're all right, and they're watching us.

"There has to be sad times in all our lives, I guess, but it's pretty hard to take. You've got to be tough. If you're going to do anything like this, you've got to be real strong and have faith that things are going to be okay."

A covenant of understanding persists between the wagon drivers and their families. "You hear it from the wagon drivers themselves," Tara suggests. "They all say, 'Well, at least he died doing something he loved to do.'" Richard Cosgrave lived the life he wanted, Tom emphasizes. "Richard loved it. He absolutely lived to go down the road, and to have the horses around and to be around them. It was a shared love. It was so flukey that you never really blame the sport for it. I never hated the horses or hated the wagons. It was an accident, and it happened."

Following Richard's funeral, Tara returned to run the Hands Hills ranch with her sons, managing 130 breeding cows on two and a half sections. "Many people said they wouldn't have been able to stay there and do it, but to me it was the easy way out. Instead of having to make any major decisions, move somewhere, or do something different, I just carried on. One day went into the next. I didn't know where else to go, anyway. It doesn't matter where you go. It's not going to make it any better. It kind of felt good being there [on the ranch]."

But, Tara admits, "It was hard at first. You learn a lot. Richard and I had done it all together, so I kind of knew what to do and how to do it. We'd also just bought a young cattle herd, so I didn't have to sell off old cows. That made it easier, too." Tara's neighbors also helped enormously, offering assistance throughout the year.

Tara stayed on the farm in Hand Hills for seven years, until her son Chad finished school. "Colt decided he wanted to run the ranch, and I didn't want to anymore, so I sold it to Colt. It was a big step. It was hard to drive out the lane. But with Colt being there, it's still like home. I can still go back." She moved in with Ross Nelson at his ranch near Milo, Alberta. Nelson is the nephew of legendary driver Lloyd Nelson, and he, too, is a former chuckwagon outrider and driver, and a long-time friend from the chuckwagon circuit. "It was a good move for all of us," Tara states.

Despite losing their father, Tara's sons continued with their interest in wagon racing. The summer following Richard's accident, "As soon as the kids were out of school," Tara says, "they both wanted to go to the races. They loved it."

Chad started working as a hired man for Norm Cuthbertson, a close friend who had lived with Richard and Tara for ten years. Colt moved to High River and began training horses with his uncle Tom and cousin Jason. Fans and friends asked Tara, "How can you let your kids do it?" She replies, "My answer to that is the kids never asked for permission. It [chuckwagon racing] is a good life. It's something we've got them interested in all their life, and to tell them they can't do it or they shouldn't do it . . . As bad as it's been for us, it's also been a great life. It's very family-oriented. We couldn't tell them not to do it. But I told them to do it, because they wanted to do it, and not because it needs to be carried on for the generations."

While her sons dove into the sport, Tara says, "With losing Richard, I lost a whole way of life. We had one field where the horses came in behind the barn, right up to the kitchen window. Even just not having the horses at home was a big, big difference."

For her, a permanent connection to the sport had been lost. "Now it's very different for me. To this day I still love to sit and watch the races, but I'm not there day after day, all the time. The horses aren't mine any-more. I used to have a reason to be there, and that definitely changed to where I'm more of a visitor. I'm watching; I'm not involved the same way I was. I go to every race to watch the kids, but I drive to watch the races and then I go home."

Seeing her sitting in the stands, fans still marvel at her resiliency. They ask her, "How can you watch your kids?" She replies, "I guess, over the years, you've watched a million races, and so seldom does anything happen. Even now, I don't watch them thinking something is going to. If it does, I guess you deal with it, but you don't watch them thinking that. You're maybe just a little more nervous or tense about it."

Tara's most dreaded evening came when Chad and Colt first raced together. Colt drove and Chad outrode behind him. Tara flew to Grande Prairie to watch the race, which turned out to be uneventful. She laughs. "I was more scared when Chad got his driver's license and went into town Friday night in his truck. He wrecked a couple of those. That was more nerve-wracking than watching him outride."

Tara has confidence in her sons' abilities. "Colt really learned how to drive with Tom and Jason. He's a driver who stays out of trouble. He's cau-tious until he drives the same horses long enough so he knows what they are going to do. Then he adds aggressiveness to the caution, which you have to do. He doesn't get very excited."

For the first time since Richard won the Calgary Stampede's aggregate time in 1993, the Cosgrave name returned to the Rangeland Derby in 2001. Twenty-three-year-old Colt Cosgrave was the first wagon driver to compete who had four generations of drivers on both his mother's and father's sides.

When Richard Cosgrave died, Tom Glass lost not only a brother-in-law, but also his best friend. In a 1993 interview, Tom said, "I didn't know it was possible to love another man, but it is. I have a lot of people in my life, but there'll never be another guy in my life like Richard Cosgrave." Richard lived with Tom from age fifteen till he married Tara, and Tom and Richard stood as best man at each other's weddings. "He was just a good guy. He was always happy, always smiling. He always had a grin."

Losing Richard, Tom says, "took a lot out of wagon racing for me. Since Richard was killed, it never was the same. It's probably half the reason why I'm retired. If he was still here and racing, I'd probably still be racing. We trained together, we travelled together. Out of the one hundred new cows he had the year he died, thirty of them were mine. We were just great friends. I miss him a lot. Over our fireplace, it's his picture that's over the mantel — nobody else's."

The losses of family and friends in wagon racing have not been easy for Tom. "Actually, it's the only bad thing of my whole life. I've had a great life, except for Rod, Richard, and George [driver George Normand, killed in a wagon race in 1994]. It couldn't have been worse. Rod was my best buddy and little brother, and Richard was my best friend. It's a terrible thing to say, but one thing I probably got out of Rod's death is I probably haven't believed in God ever since that day. I just quit — I lost it. I just figured, if he's there, he ain't doing a very good job. If he is there, I don't like him anyways. When they're eighteen, it's just too young. That's not fair."

He adds, "You go on with it, but you never entirely get over it. I think about them guys all the time. When we went on holidays to Mexico [in 2000], Tara and driver Doyle Mullaney were down there, and we talked about Richard every other day. It's cool — he'll always be around."

After George Normand's accident, a Toronto reporter cornered Tom. "He asked me, 'How do you justify people dying in the wagon business? How many people have you lost? What justifies you to keep racing?'" Tom appreciates that outsiders don't understand, but, he replies, "How many people have been killed on Calgary's Deerfoot Trail [a busy city thoroughfare] in the last ten years? More people die driving on their way to work than on the racetrack. They don't close it down. If I'm going to quit wagon racing, then I'm going to quit driving on Deerfoot, too. And I'm going to quit getting on airplanes. Maybe if we weren't driving wagons, we'd be racing motorcycles or whatever."

In 1998, in the thick of the chuckwagon season, Tom Glass decided to retire. Many fans were surprised. Mandatory retirement is at age sixty-five, and at fifty Tom seemed too young to shut 'er down. "In Edmonton they've got us in a little compound there — locked in," he explains. "We're behind a wire fence, we are all touching each other, and we're jammed in with a bunch of equipment. There's about ten extra square feet per person. It was probably 80 above, a beautiful sunny day, and I'm sitting in this compound. I thought, 'Christ, this is like being in jail.' I'm in the middle of this city, I'm in this compound, looking at this wire fence, and thought, 'There's got to be more out there besides this.' I made the decision sitting on the ramp of my truck. I never talked to anybody about it. My nephew Colt just walked by, and I said, 'Tell them guys over there these horses are for sale. I'm done.' He looked at me and said, 'Oh yeah, sure.' He didn't believe it, but the next day I started selling horses."

As one of the sport's reigning superstars, Tom startled the entire wagon community with his decision. "I quit because I got tired of going up and down the road every summer: Ponoka July first, Calgary in July, High River in June, every town the same time. I wanted to do something else. I'd been going every year since I was ten years old, and I thought, 'I'm still young enough. I can still compete. I can still team rope and still win rodeos.' I just wanted to do something different.

"I think my wife was happy about [my retirement]," Tom says. "She went up and down the road with me for twenty years. But I think she was probably the only one. I know my mom wasn't." When Tom told Iris in Edmonton, she said, "No, you're not quitting."

Tom says, "Mom didn't believe me; I know she didn't. But I said, 'Sorry, Ma.' She took it pretty hard. She didn't say too much, but I know she didn't like it." He laughs and adds, "Mom gave me hell a few times. She said I was too young to retire."

After Tom announced his intention, fellow wagon drivers also tried to reverse his decision. "Jerry Bremner said, 'We need you in the business. We can't afford to lose guys like you.' It was a great compliment, coming from another wagon driver. Even Kelly [Sutherland] said, 'You can't quit. Stick around for another couple of years and then we'll all go.' I don't know. Something just clicked, and I had had enough."

When Tom's thirty-three year driving career ended, he says, "One of the neatest things was the day I retired, at Strathmore, in 1998. I won the day money; I thought that was kind of a nice way to end it. As I came back in front of the grandstand, before the announcer even started to say anything, people started to stand up. They all stood up and gave me a standing ovation. My last race — that really hit home. And when Les McIntyre, the announcer, said, 'We're saying goodbye to one of the greatest wagon drivers of all time,' that was probably the most special moment of my whole career. When I heard that, usually they were talking about Dad or one of the old boys. It wasn't even real that he was saying that about me."

Following his retirement from wagon racing, Tom has competed actively in team roping. As a "header," Tom ropes the head of a steer, pulls left, and ensures the steer holds steady so the "heeler" can rope its hind legs. He has won several titles, and competes in the Southern U.S. every winter.

Retiree Tom's checkerboard chuckwagon is parked in front of his family's home — "a little sentimental value, I guess." He has no regrets, he says. "Wagon racing was never the same after Richard. The fun wasn't there. If Jason hadn't started around then, I don't know if I would've gone on as long as I did. I guess I miss the driving, spring training, and breaking the new ones, but I don't miss going up and down the road."

Tom's life changed when he lost the people he loved. But he does not second-guess the life he chose; it has been a satisfying one. "I had a great career. I had a lot of good horses, I made a lot of good friends, and I made some money. It's always amazed me that people go to work on Monday and they wish it was Friday. They go to work at eight o'clock in the morning and wish it was five at night. To me that's just wishing your life away. You're better to quit and do something different, even for half the money. You're not here long enough. I just hate to see people wishing it away."

Fans still ask Tom, "Your dad won Calgary four times. How many times did you win?" But he replies, "That doesn't mean anything to me. I mean, I love to win, but I don't think, 'It's how many times?' I love that I won Calgary, and it was exciting, and I won the World, and it was exciting, but I'm not into numbers." Rather than records, Tom is proudest of his ability to break horses. "I always broke my own horses and kept my own."

The only other broken horses Tom acquired were Richard Cosgrave's lead team, Faith and Duddy, which he bought from Tara after Richard was killed. "They were probably as good of a lead team that I ever drove. They were awesome. They were like power steering." Tom won the 1994 Calgary Stampede with Faith and Duddy. After the race, he knew it should have been Richard holding the trophy and the $50,000 cheque. Standing on stage, Tom said, "This one's for Richard."

When Tom retired, he gave Faith and Duddy to his nephew Colt. That August, Colt took Faith to Dawson Creek. On the show's last day, the final day of the season, the horse's heart stopped as he pulled up after a race. He was still in harness, and was the only horse to fall down. Faith died on August 7, the same day as Colt's father, Richard, had died. Losing the cherished horse, Tara says, "was kind of hard for everybody. But it's part of it; it always has been. You get over it."

For the Glasses, wagon racing again proved that it is about more than just leather and horseflesh. Their faith is larger than one great horse. Their devotion lies at the heart of the sport — with the family and friends who sustain and share their dreams. Their memories are woven into the family's saddle blankets, and their love echoes around the empty racetracks.

10

Jason the Argonaut

That's why this sport is so unique. If it was easy, everybody would be doing it. There aren't many wagon drivers in this world, and I think that's for a reason. It's not the easiest life or the easiest sport to do.
— JASON GLASS

Finding Jason Glass on the racetrack is easy. Just watch for a cowboy looking for his hat. Usually, after a wagon race, an outrider or race official can be seen retrieving Jason's cowboy hat. "I've got a small head and a weird-shaped head," he explains, "so I can't keep a hat on my head during a race. My hat falls off every race — I go through a lot of hats. I finally found a felt hat that would stay on. I used it for about four years, but it got beat up. It was a terrible-looking, ugly hat, but I wore it, because I could keep it on my head." He adds, "I tried putting one of them idiot straps around my throat to hold my hat on. I got bugged about that too much, so I took it off. Now I just let my hat fly off, and if I get it back, I get it back."

Hat flying, Jason Glass has carried the family name and its wagon enterprises into the twenty-first century. He was the sport's first ever fourth-generation driver. And like his father and uncles, Jason's most important education happened on the High River farm. Growing up in Okotoks, fifteen miles away, Jason tried to visit Iris and Ron every weekend.

"All week I thought about coming out to the farm and playing with the horses." Jason owned a black-and-white pony named Checkers. In the winter, the young cowboy harnessed a small toboggan to Checkers and drove him around the farm. He laughs, "He'd run around the fields, tip me over, and just stand there. I'd go catch him, jump on the toboggan, and go. In the summer I'd ride him, but he'd buck me off six times a day."

As children, Jason and his friends often played chuckwagon. Their games were the same ones that Tom and his friends had played twenty years earlier. "At the Calgary Stampede," Jason says, "we'd steal shopping carts and push each other around barrels. We'd also put three real wagons together side by side, get up in the wagon seats, get our lines, and drive those wagons with pretend horses all day long."

Jason was naturally comfortable around horses, and only once does he recall being scared by the family business. The Glasses were racing in Morris, Manitoba, and, "Dale, Dad's wheel horse, got pulling back in the stall. He pulled back and then dove forward like they do when the horses are confused or scared. I was a little kid up in the manger, and Dale kept jumping up on me. The horse wasn't hurting me, but I was panicking. I remember Dad was standing there, and he wasn't too concerned about it. It is the one memory where I maybe questioned getting involved. Other than that, in the back of my mind I knew I was eventually going to do it."

At age twelve, Jason moved with his family to their new house on the High River farm. "From then on, in my mind, it was full-on wagons. I decided I was going to be an outrider and then a wagon driver." At age fourteen, he outrode for an EXPO 86 exhibition race at Hand Hills, Alberta.

Recalling his initiation, Jason says, "It was the first time I actually competed as an outrider. I got through the race, but had a runaway at the end. I muscled around the track three times, because I wasn't strong enough to stop my horse." By age sixteen, however, Jason could handle and manoeuvre an outriding horse. Gordon Stewart hired him to outride in Grande Prairie. At the next show, Jason began riding behind his father. A month later, Tom's outfit won the 1987 Calgary Stampede. Jason won as a rookie outrider, just as his father had done.

Besides having a talent for outriding, Jason was also a skilled hockey player. In 1991, with the Calgary Royals, he won the Junior A Tier II Alberta championship. "I was a corner man — I roughed it in the corner. But I decided I didn't want to drop my gloves for the rest of my life, playing hockey. Ninety percent of our team got a scholarship to go play somewhere. I could've gone to school and played hockey, or I could get into the movie business. The movie business was lucrative at that time, and it perfectly fit in with wagon racing. So I decided that was the end of my hockey."

Jason did not transfer the hockey superstitions of his teammates to his wagon career. "I've seen too many hockey players who can't do things without doing them in a certain way. It drives them nuts. I'll never believe in that. I'm sure there are wagon drivers who are superstitious, but to me it seems like too much of a pain in the ass to worry about it. You've got enough things on your mind to let superstitions get in there."

As a young outrider, Jason focused his dreams on driving a chuckwagon professionally. His ambitions began early. When his dad would finish a race, he says, "As long as I could hang off the back of the wagon's stove rack, I'd climb in and be on the seat with Dad. I was doing it by age six. I was always trying to grab the lines out of his hands. He gave me two lines and I'd drive two horses back from the grandstand. Eventually, he gave me all four."

When they are racing, cowboys must instinctively know which lines are in their hands. There is no time to look or think about what line they need. Tom says, "You can't look up and down to see which line you're grabbing. It's got to be a natural reaction, or you are too late. It's like a piano player — he knows where every key is. If you play with the lines long enough, you'll know exactly where they are." To train Jason, Tom says, "We used to tie a bungee cord on his lines to the side of a liner. Jason would sit in the wagon and change lines. He'd reach over and pick up the line needed for a horse, let it go, reach to the other hand, and grab that line."

As Jason's mentor, Tom shaped Jason's wagon education. Like his father, Ron, Tom was a silent teacher, leading by example. Jason says, "That probably was the best way to go about teaching me. I guess I'm a little bit stubborn. Our whole family is kind of that way; we don't like to be told what to do. We like to learn things on our own. You can't be forced to do anything . . . with our family, anyway."

Jason was driving four up by age thirteen. To help him practice, Tom recalls, "I hooked four of my outriding horses up and gave Jason the lines. Those horses were awful to drive. That's why they were outriding horses. One would go one way, and one the other." Jason worked the outriding horses for two weeks, repeatedly turning barrels. Tom laughs. "Finally, one morning Jason said, *"Hyaw!"* and threw the lines at them. All four horses just stood there and looked at him. They had had enough. They weren't going anymore."

The influence of Tom's training is pronounced in Jason's driving. The Glass style, the body language, have been passed on to him. Iris says, "Tom, Ron, and Jason all drive exactly the same. Exactly. It's the same position. Jason just looks like his dad, and Tom just looked like his dad. They get their leg up in one corner and lean over a certain way into the turn with their whole body. You can just see it as plain as can be. It's hereditary, and from practicing, riding, and watching it all their lives."

Chuckwagon youngsters often mimic their family predecessors. Iris adds, "Colt [Cosgrave] also drives just like his dad, Richard." The Cosgraves are famous for bouncing in their seats as they race. In fact, Richard Cosgrave's father was known as "Bouncing Bobby." Iris laughs. "I told Colt not to bounce too hard, because he's really big and he'll break the seat."

Jason's driving thrills came early in his wagon career. During his second year, Jason says, "One race I'll never forget featured my Uncle Richard, Dad, and myself in a three-wagon heat. It was probably the first time I got into a later heat with the good wagon drivers. I was in the middle of those two guys and they were running really tight on me. They always ran tight, because they'd been racing for so long. Dad was on the outside and Richard was on the inside. They were rubbing my wheels from both sides. I was scared to death. I didn't know what the hell to do or where to go, so I just carried on. She was awful close all the way around the track. I got into tight quarters and hit the panic button. Nothing got hurt, but I was definitely spooked. I'd never been in a spot like that."

Following the race, Jason was furious at both his dad and his uncle, and he refused to participate in the post-race parade in front of the crowd. He laughs. "I remember wanting to punch both of them. I never did hit either one of them, but I was excited as hell. I jumped off the seat and was screaming mad when they came back. I think they were surprised I got that excited about the whole deal. To them it was probably not even a big deal. They bugged me for being a suck and not going back in front of the crowd. They said, 'Deal with it, kid.'"

Later, in Strathmore, Jason turned the nervous tables on his uncle Richard. Jason borrowed Richard's horse Pokey, a right-hand leader. "Richard only loaned horses to my dad. His horses were his pets. He wouldn't even watch my race, because I was driving his favorite horse." During the race, Jason made a solid barrel turn and took the lead. "I was out front. I was running good." As he bounded around the second corner, he lost sight of the end of his lines. They were hanging over the side of his wagon box and they hooked onto the wagon wheel's grease nipple. "The lines wrapped around the wheel and just literally stopped my whole outfit. One horse fell down, it sucked on him so bad. The whole outfit stopped — *right now!*

"Richard was listening on the intercom and heard, 'Jason Glass's horses went down on the second corner,' so I imagine he had more of a heart attack than I did." The horses were unhurt and, once the lines were untangled, Jason walked them back to the barn. "Richard was such a jokester that, once he knew the horses were okay, he was laughing. He knew I had had a good turn, I was out in front, and then disaster struck. I never finished running the race, and he got a kick out of that."

In all his wrecks, both in competition and at home, Jason asserts, "It's surprising — probably 90 percent of the time, no horses get hurt. Because they're big, strong, and fast animals, it looks violent and scary, but it's never as bad as it looks. The horses might fall down, but very rarely do they get hurt." He compares wagon horses to track athletes. During a track race, he says, "One guy trips another guy, they all fall down, and they get up. There might be some skin off their knees, but that's it. It's no different with the horses. The horses jump right up and forget all about it." Jason continues, "I've never been in that many big wrecks — just minor ones where no one gets hurt. I've been fortunate that way. I've never broken anything on a wagon."

Although he was never seriously hurt racing, Jason has had to deal with numerous training runaways. Often a line breaks. Then, he says, "all you can do is guide the horses into a bush or to the side of a building and stop whatever is going on." One day, as he was driving a wagon horse on the two-wheeled training cart, a line on the harness snapped. Jason and his horse were off and running. "I started turning him in a circle and got him stopped. But he kicked over a tug and just kept kicking. He pulled me forward with the lines and kicked me in the face. I went down, and I was knocked out for a moment or two. Then the horse started backing up, pushing the cart up over me. Dad came out, got the cart off me, and I came to. Everything was all right. My teeth kind of went through my lips. There was no permanent damage, but it was a scary moment for a few minutes. That stuff happens, and all you can do is stay far enough back that hopefully you don't get hurt to an extreme," Jason laughs. "A guy wants to always keep his head away from their feet as much as possible."

To ease the responsibilities of running a large wagon-racing team, Jason and his cousin Colt Cosgrave live, work, and travel together. From April to August, Colt moves into High River from his Hand Hills ranch. Together the two men carry on the family's practical style of apprenticeship. Jason is eight years older, and it is his turn to loan horses to a family member.

Jason explains, "Colt's trying to build up his herd. It's easier to break into the sport and travel with someone who has all the equipment and horses. It works for me, too, because I've got somebody breaking my horses in an actual race. I don't have to drive the new ones and experiment; I just stick with the old boys that work and sub in with new horses. Sometimes it's not fair to Colt, because he drives and breaks the new horses. I steal them and he starts again, but that's just how it works. That's how I did it with my dad, and that's how everyone does it until you start owning enough. Until I started buying horses, I didn't have a say in what I drove. That's just how it works.

"It's a big operation in terms of horses. In the springtime we'll train forty to forty-five horses and pack twenty-seven down the road — that's two liners with two of us driving. But it's necessary now everyone's buying a bunch of horses, and good ones. It used to be that everybody worked on one outfit — four horses. Now I want two outfits just as strong as each other, and then backups."

During training, Tom helps Jason and Colt. Jason says, "Dad goes right back to the basics. We'd make our laps and he'd say, 'Take this outfit to the opposite end of the field.' Dad compared our training to my grandfather's, and Grandpa always went into the far stubble field a mile down the lane." Ron Glass trained his one outfit for sixty to ninety minutes, unlike the thirty minutes Jason spends with an outfit. "Grandpa would walk the horses two miles, make them stand, and drive them like an old farm team. He'd make them really behave themselves and let them get comfortable with what they're doing. Dad reminded me to do that.

"We drive seven to nine outfits a day, and if you did that with every outfit you'd run out of daylight. But every now and then, certain outfits and certain horses need that. A guy forgets. You get caught up with the number of horses and the time of day. You don't slow down to actually give the horses what maybe they do need. Dad slowed us down with those horses. At the Hand Hills ranch, my uncle Richard Cosgrave used to take his outfit and park them in the slough — just sit there. He'd have a cigarette, a beer, whatever, and sit there for twenty minutes. Then he'd drive out and carry on with the training. Things like that are unheard-of nowadays."

Jason feels that today's faster-trained horses may not be as mentally strong. His grandfather's horses knew completely what was expected of them. "On our farm, we try to stay with how it used to be. We've still got the track out in the field, and we also drive in different fields. I don't ever want to get away from that. In the back of my mind, I try to stick with how the old boys trained. To me, they did it for a reason."

All year round, horses bind the Glass family together. They spend more time living and working with each other than most families. They rely on each other, and they are very close. Their unity, their alliance, and their mutual ambitions stir up strong emotions.

To illustrate, Jason's most heart-pounding, emotion-filled, sensational race occurred in 1997. He and Tom were racing together in the Calgary Stampede final. It was Jason's first appearance in the Stampede's Dash for Cash. And it was only the second father–son match-up to occur in the final heat [the first was Allan and Buddy Bensmiller in 1979]. Two checkered wagons were about to race for the bronze trophy. Iris reflects, "I always said, 'One day I'm going to have Tom and Jason in the final heat.' I did it in '97. It was the greatest feeling in the world. It was marvellous."

To qualify for the tenth-night's race, Jason had to make up three seconds on the ninth evening. "I barely made it in. After taking penalties at the beginning of the week, I climbed back up the ladder. The ninth night, I had a really fast time, and the guy who was in fourth didn't." He recalls listening to the radio in the barns. "When they announced that I'd made the final, I didn't know if it was really possible, because there was such a gap. I snuck in by thirteen one-hundredths of a second. That was exciting. With Dad in the race as well, it was a dream come true. It didn't really matter who won the race; we both got to race against each other for the fifty." Tom adds, "After Jason and I made it to the final heat, I said, 'It doesn't matter what happens; we both had an awesome week.'"

Fans might assume that Jason and Tom formulated a plan to ensure that one of them won. But Jason says, "I think we had a deal to split the money for whoever did get there. 'A thirty-twenty split on the fifty.' That was kind of a joke before we even got in. Other than that, it was just *go for it*. You can't really plan a strategy out on the track between two guys. Once the horn blows, you're racing against the other three guys."

Before the race, the Glasses' sponsors passed out black-and-white checkered flags in the grandstand. Iris recalls, "When those two checker-board wagons came in together, the crowd just went *nuts.*" She was cheering from the rodeo chutes. "People always asked me, 'Who did you yell for?' And I said, 'I yelled for both of them: *Come on, you checkers!*'"

Tom and Jason were hooked against Buddy Bensmiller and Kelly Sutherland. In the draw for barrel positions, Bensmiller drew Barrel 1, Sutherland pulled Barrel 4, Tom had Barrel 2, and Jason was left with Barrel 3. Pulling up in front of the grandstand, Jason recalls, "It was kind of nerve-wracking, with the noise and the flags. Normally, you don't even see that stuff. In the practice turns it was overwhelming how loud it was. And the checkered flags! Even if you tried not to see them, I could see them that night. It was something else."

Jason tried to maintain his composure as he completed his practice turns. As usual, he wanted complete command of his horses. "I wanted everything lined up nice and straight. I didn't want any horse out of control or goofing off. It can throw everything out of whack, make another horse mad, or break my concentration. Some guys like to drive fast or have crazy practice turns, but my dad and I, we've always gone nice and slow, having complete control of all four horses. I try to do that every night. Nothing is frustrated, spooked, or stepped on. It pays off when nothing is ramming and jamming. Everything is nice and straight, and all four horses are pulling. And it saves time when the horn goes. Everything is focused and paying attention, instead of goofing off and messing around. The horses are right in front of you and ready to go straight ahead."

Jason recounts the race's start. "One horse moved right before the horn. I think I was just too nervous. I kind of slipped, fell down in my box, and all hell broke loose. I hit the top barrel and got that first fifty [the prize money] out of the way."

From Barrel 4, Kelly Sutherland made a spectacular barrel turn, stole the rail position, and led the race from start to finish. Bensmiller finished second, Tom third, and Jason fourth. "After the race we had a beer," Jason says. "What happens, happens — you just carry on. A guy's been in a lot of races, and it either works or it doesn't. I knew going into the race that I might have a little trouble with that outfit on the short barrels. I could've got lucky and had everything work out, but if they do it once, there's a good chance the same thing will happen again. Usually, you've got to go with the horses that got you there. If you try to change too much, it will always backfire."

Since Jason began driving in 1989, he had not won his hometown show at High River — the North American Chuckwagon Championship. "I always had trouble racing in High River." That changed on a stormy night in June 2000.

After a week of rain, the track was heavy and gooey. During the Dash for Cash, lightning flashed in the northwest. "I don't mind those nights," Jason says. "It's kind of fun and a major challenge. If you have a good run in the mud and your animals win a race, you know they've got big hearts. It's pretty easy to walk away from the mud, have an average night, and blame it on the weather. It's something else to conquer it."

For Jason, winning the show was "a huge monkey off my back. I'll probably never forget it. I was so focused that week to get it done. It seemed like a period in my life where I really did put a big effort into it, and it paid off." When his outfit sloshed down the homestretch, he says, "Crossing the finish line is what a guy remembers. It is the biggest rush. It is a big relief when you finally know you've accomplished it. It's like, 'Thank you.'"

He explains his indebtedness: "You thank whoever got a guy there. Whether it's family, friends, or the Big Guy in the sky — whoever put it all together, the reason that it happened. It's a big group of people to thank, and you can never thank them all — sponsors, family, friends, and horses. It's definitely not the guy driving the wagon."

Jason never feels that he was pressured to win races or championships. "I was always told, 'You won't win anything for ten years.' The first time I won a show was at Trout Springs [a former racetrack near Calgary], and it was my tenth year." He admits, though, that he "felt a little pressure as a kid to carry on and to be in the sport. I think the young guys [from chuckwagon families] may have some pressure to actually compete, but not to do well, because the sport is so tough to do."

A bachelor, and with no future Glass cowboys and cowgirls yet forthcoming, Jason reveals, "Now I've got the pressure to have some more generations. 'Where are the kids?' That's probably the biggest pressure I've ever had — to make the sport go on past me."

Following High River, Jason attained a lifelong goal and won the World championship in 2000. It was his first, and the eighth World title won by a Glass driver. "Above anything Calgary offers, winning the World is the biggest accomplishment in wagon racing. Calgary is ten nights, but it's still a barrel-draw to win that last heat. The World is the total combined points of every night, all the whole summer, except for Calgary. Over the season there are so many events, so many nights of racing. The World is the most cherished, the most remembered reward, and I think it's the hardest thing to achieve. Winning the World is the proudest achievement I could ever reach."

Jason was awarded his championship buckle and bronze trophy at the World Professional Chuckwagon Association's 2000 banquet. Standing up in front of his peers and friends, he says, "It was a moment, that's for sure.

A guy gets a little choked up talking in front of all those people who you have respected and watched your whole life — all of the wagon drivers who have won it. That was a big moment." During any individual's lifetime, Jason emphasizes, "you don't often get something that means so much to you. How many times does a human get to speak about something that means so much to them in front of people?"

"Jason and his dad are really close," says Iris. "Oh God, they're close. As Jason gave the speech, he said, 'I'd like to give credit to a couple of people that made me come this far and helped me win this championship. One is my grandma. She is the backbone of our whole outfit. She helps me hitch, she helps me doctor, and she helps watch the horses, making sure they're fed when I'm gone. And the other big helper is my dad, Thomas.' Tom is wiping great big tears coming out of his eyes, and he says, 'I know when that kid calls me Thomas, he has the greatest idea of what I am to him of anybody in the world.' There wasn't a dry eye at our table."

Jason laughs, "In a way, it was nice to get the speech over with. But I'd do it again — that's for sure!"

Jason inherited his father's motivation to win. "I've always been competitive, and I think our whole family's been that way. To try and achieve excellence in a sport is kind of natural. Whatever I can do from year to year to improve with my horses and my crew — that's the fun part of it for me. I don't carry on being a wagon driver just to do it. I want to put absolutely everything I can into the sport, and make it grow and evolve."

No matter where he is in the standings or what the quality of his horses, Jason consistently pushes himself. "To be competitive is to get the most out of your horses, night to night. If I come off Barrel 3, and there are two guys on my inside who will barrel with me, the potential is I could be three wide and third in the race. Yet my outfit has run the best race they could run. That's 'competitive' to me.

"If I'm on Barrel 1 and my outfit's been really crackin' and working, if they're on top of their game, I know I could be first. And if I come back to the barn and had a bad race, because I missed a line or didn't drive like I figure I should've, then it's frustrating. The nights you get really pissed off or frustrated are when you screw up yourself — you drop a line, you're not quite focused, or you're still hungover from the night before."

Jason recalls a time he returned to the barns feeling disappointed. At the 2000 Ponoka Stampede, he used a new wheel horse. At the horn, the wheeler charged so hard that he ran over the leader. "They got tangled up and my outfit fell down in the infield." Jason received a "no time" and trotted his outfit back to the barns. "I couldn't get it out of my mind that if one of the old boys, like Dad or Dallas Dorchester, was in the wagon, they could have got the horses out of the infield and completed the race. Maybe they would have felt it or seen it sooner than I did and been able to deal with it. They would have got it done, just out of experience."

However, Jason admits, "There are so many variables. Whether you're in the top three or top ten, it all depends on your horses, everyone else's horses, and track conditions. I think it's impossible to say every night, 'I'll be first,' or even third or fifth. But if you can be in the top five or top ten every night in one summer, you're going to be in the top three at the end."

Jason's ambitions are intertwined with his family's legacy. At the 2001 Calgary Stampede, Jason had the show's lowest aggregate time. Standing on stage with Iris and family, he accepted the Richard Cosgrave Memorial Trophy, named in honor of his deceased uncle. Jason's tears flowed as his aunt Tara presented the bronze trophy.

The following night, Jason raced in the Rangeland Derby's championship heat. Bellowing to his horses, Jason's outfit charged from behind to beat Kelly Sutherland's wagon to the wire. But one of Jason's outriders was late, and Sutherland won the championship. It was one of the most sensational finishes in Stampede history.

Already a World champion, Jason has just reached his prime. He has only just begun winning. He is one of the sport's new leaders. And, as proud bearer of the family's torch and driver of the checkered wagon, he has not yet finished learning and improving: "I'm going to get better. I have to get better."

11

Rolling with the Punches

The old theory is, if two guys come into an intersection and see each other, usually both guys hit the brakes and there's a big crash. But if one guy out of the two hits the gas, there probably won't be a crash. That's the stunt guy — he'll hit the gas. I hit the gas to get out of a wreck. That's the way we try to live with the stunts.
— TOM GLASS

As long as the Glass family has been racing wagons, they have been falling out of them — on purpose. It started with Tom Lauder. During a 1925 Calgary Stampede race, Tom's chuckwagon hit a barrel, twisted, and flipped a complete somersault. Filmmaker and actor Hoot Gibson was in the city filming *The Calgary Stampede*. After seeing the spectacular wreck, Gibson asked Lauder if he could repeat it in front of a movie camera. Lauder said, "Sure," and for $200 — more money than Lauder would have earned if he had won the Stampede — Tom performed the family's first filmed stunt.

Movies were filmed in Alberta intermittently for the next fifty years.

And when productions did arrive, the Glasses were involved. In the 1940s, for the film *Northwest Stampede,* Ron Glass drove his chuckwagon and Iris rode as an outrider. In the film's climactic final race, the wagon's back wheel falls off. Ron and his chuckwagon were also cast in the film *Old Hacksaw*. The movie's story followed a horse and its various jobs, including jumping, flat racing, and running on Ron's chuckwagon.

In the late 1960s, the production of *Little Big Man,* starring Dustin Hoffman, came to Alberta. It was the first motion picture that Reg Glass worked on. "They needed some guys to ride in the cavalry, shooting Indians, and I applied for it." It was also the first major film experience for the Glasses' friend John Scott, who is now the major supplier of horses and wagons to the Alberta film industry.

For *Little Big Man,* a scene was shot in –35°F weather. "The soldiers attacked and massacred an Indian village," Reg remembers. "We took what wardrobe they gave us and adapted it for the cold weather situation. The director was really happy that we had scarves tied on our hats and over our ears. The tough thing was that I had a single-shot rifle, and I had to keep reloading it, which was awfully cold on the hands."

Recalling his first film experiences, Tom Glass says, "I owned a store in Okotoks, selling western clothes and boots. I got to know John Scott, and he asked me if I'd be interested in working on *Pioneer Woman.*" The movie was filmed in Waterton Lakes National Park, and Tom drove a team of oxen. He next worked as a wrangler for the Walt Disney film *The Boy Who Talked to Badgers,* filmed near Drumheller.

In the mid-1970s, when director Robert Altman's *Buffalo Bill and the Indians* arrived in Alberta, the entire family was hired. Even preschooler Jason and his sister, Corry, were cast as extras. Reg remembers, "*Buffalo Bill and the Indians* was just a riot. We had so much fun." Emulating Buffalo Bill's original show, the cowboys created a Wild West extrava-ganza. "There were thirty cowboys working full-time, wranglers and rodeo ex-champions. We did all kinds of neat stuff. One big American bulldogged a buffalo. Nobody said he could do it, but he did it."

Reg drove the stagecoach during Buffalo Bill's grand entry. His father rode shotgun, and Iris followed on horseback. "I was a brave cowboy," Iris says. "I had a man's outfit on — chaps, and a big six-gun on my hip." In one pageantry-filled scene, hundreds of extras stood along the camp's main street as Buffalo Bill's troupe paraded by. Iris drove a horse and buggy, and Reg again drove a stagecoach.

"Dad had harnessed up the horses," Reg recalls. "The lead team was really juicy and pulling, and one wheel horse was jumping, bucking, and screwing around. The wheeler bailed around, threw a fit, and took all the skin off between my fingers [where Reg was holding the lines]." With all the people lined up along the street, he says, "I was scared to death these horses would get away on me. I kept saying, 'Jesus Christ, what's wrong with that goddam horse?' We get towards the end of the street, and my old man says, 'I thought he was going pretty good.'

"I said, 'What do you mean, 'pretty good'?

"He said, 'Well, that's the first time he's ever been hitched up.'

"I said, 'What the hell are you talking about?'

"He said, 'Well, that other horse was a little sore. This one looked like a match, so I put him in there.'"

Reg laughs. "I could've killed him."

Paul Newman starred as Buffalo Bill. Iris recalls, "We played volleyball between shots with Paul Newman. I always got really close to him to hit the ball, so I could run into him and touch him. That's when he was in his prime." She laughs, "Somebody asked me, 'How did you do, playing with him?' I said, 'Oh boy, it was good. But I sure did a lot of fumbling running into him.'"

Reg performed his first stunt in the movie. "I jumped off my horse to the top of the stagecoach. Other guys couldn't figure out how to do it, so I went back to my chuckwagon experience. As an outrider, I always rode with really short stirrups, jockey style. I snuck over and jacked my stirrups back up. Then I just rode along beside the stagecoach and jumped out of my stirrups. They got me up another foot, so I could get to the top."

Tom shared stagecoach-driving duties with Reg. *Buffalo Bill and the Indians* was also the first film for which Tom received a stunt cheque.

"That's when I learned it was more lucrative to be a stuntman than a wrangler." As a wrangler, Tom had saddled horses and led them to the movie sets. "They'd bring an American in from Los Angeles, and I'd hand him the horse. He'd ride out on the prairie and fall off. I'd go catch the horse. The American made a thousand dollars and I made a hundred. It didn't take me long to figure out I had to fall off a horse, too." Tom adds, "They used to bring all American stunt guys to Canada, and we were the wranglers. They made all the big money, and we did all the work."

While wrangling for the American stuntmen, Tom probed them for trade secrets. "They loved to tell us how to do stuff. They weren't worried about us taking their jobs. Over a coffee we'd ask them, 'How do you do that? How do you do this?' They'd tell us and we'd listen. They'd go home, and we'd go home and practice. Now we've taken their jobs."

Opportunities were blossoming in the Canadian film industry. Tom Glass, another Albertan, and four British Columbians formed Stunts Canada, which is now Canada's largest professional stunt organization. Its talented fifty members include bull riders, kick boxers, high-fallers, and motocross racers. Reg, Tom, Jason, and Tom's daughter, Corry, are all members. Tom says, "New members don't get in it just by doing things. They have to be voted in unanimously by the other members. It's not an easy thing to get into."

When Stunts Canada began, U.S. Immigration blocked Canadians from working in the United States, but Americans could work freely in Canada. Stunts Canada pressured the Canadian government, and, Tom says, "We started closing the border a little bit. The producers couldn't bring an American up if a Canadian could do the job. Now we pretty well have full control of the border. There are still Americans who come in to do stunts, but it has to be a specialty thing, because there are so many qualified stunt guys in Canada now. It's seldom we need an American."

Cowboys and cowgirls have always excelled at stunts. Ever since the era of Tom Mix and the early oaters, cowboys have demonstrated the necessary grit, fortitude, and dexterity to succeed in the film industry. The Glass family is no exception. Their childhoods on horseback gave them the skills needed in front of the camera — they perform naturally in the saddle. Reg explains, "If you don't learn how to ride when you are a kid, it's absolutely, unbelievably hard to be a competent rider.

"These actors, when they come into a western, they're asked if they can ride. 'Well, yeah,' they'll say, because they can put a leg on each side. But they can't do anything on a horse. If a horse starts to act up, they have no idea how to handle it. If you have to worry about riding while you're riding, then you can't ride. You have to do it automatically. If actors have to do their lines *and* think about their horse, they can't do it. You lose all your timing."

Reg compares the ability to ride a horse to driving a car through city traffic. "Ask somebody if they can drive. If they can drive a car to the road and down the lane, they can 'drive.' But to drive through the middle of the city, changing radio stations, talking to somebody, and reading the traffic at the same time, then you really know how to *drive*. That's the difference. If you really know how to do something, you can do it without thinking about it."

But it is not only horsemanship that propelled the Glass family to stunt excellence. The numerous ingredients include audacity. "You've got to be a little gutsy," Tom says, "and you've got to like the adrenaline. If you don't like adrenaline, you'll make yourself sick." Also, he continues, "you've got to listen. There is nothing worse than when a stunt coordinator is talking to eight guys, and one guy is not paying attention. Ten minutes later, their life is on the line."

Jason agrees. "You don't get the job unless you pay attention. There's so much to it, including where the camera angles are and watching how your actor has walked. People that go to school don't learn it. You've got to experience it."

Stunt performers must also be willing to sacrifice their bodies. As Jason describes it, "You'll get ten jobs and people on the set will say, 'Anyone can do that.' But one job out of ten, you'll pay the price, either T-boning a car or landing on cement on your back. You pay for it. You'll question whether you'll get hurt. It takes a person that *will* do it."

Despite the risk of injury, particularly on lower-budget productions, Jason states, "If I'm the one going to do the deal and I don't think it's safe enough, it's up to me to say, 'No, I won't do the stunt.' But you may not be back — that's the chance you take. As a rule you don't say no. You make sure you're ready for it, it's calculated, and you're there to do the job. Ultimately, it's no one's fault [if an accident occurs] but your own."

The Glasses' athletic talents are also important assets in their stunt work. For example, while Tom was driving wagons, he developed his peripheral vision, training himself to compute split-second decisions. "When I was driving a wagon, I always wanted to know where the other wagon was. If I was on Barrel 2 and there was a guy on Barrel 1 and Barrel 3, on both sides, I knew where they were. I knew how close, whether they were ahead of me, and if I could take the rail. I had to know where they were. As soon as I hit the track [after turning the barrels], if I was on the 2 Barrel, I probably had less than a tenth of a second to make up my mind if I was far enough ahead to make it to the rail. If I didn't go to the rail within that tenth of a second, then [the Barrel 1 wagon] is there, and I lose it.

"I always knew where people were. That really helps in car chases, to know where that next car is without actually cranking your head and looking. You are shooting, hitting, rolling, coming up, and you've got to know where the camera is. If you're driving a car down the highway at 80 mph and there's a camera car beside you, you've got to react to it, slide the corner, and know where that other camera is out in the ditch."

Jason agrees that their sports experience has benefitted their stunt work. "After being in a wagon, the pressure on a movie set is almost non-existent. In my own, real world, I'm dealing with live animals and people's lives. The movies are all kind of fake. There's still a responsibility, but it seems less than driving a wagon. After doing wagons, standing in front of a camera, making yourself hit the ground and hitting your mark is rather easy."

The stress of stunt work is concentrated on timing and hitting marks, or targets. "Sometimes there is huge pressure," explains Jason, "because the actors are standing around making $10 million, and you're going in to double them. You can't screw up. You don't get too many chances in the movie business. If you screw up, hurt an actor, or run over a camera, your career can end in an awful hurry. The money is so big, and it's a big responsibility. So I think the wagons and our lifestyle have helped us overcome those fears and deal with it."

The Glasses focus on the action, coolly performing their jobs. "Maybe there is no replacement for the car you're driving," Reg says, "or maybe the cameras are close by and they're worth half a million dollars. Unless you've been a pro athlete or been subjected to that kind of pressure, it's very hard to do for a lot of people. Most people, when something happens, they panic — they slam on the brakes.

"Contrary to what people think, you're not worried about yourself most of the time. You're worried about doing the job. The bigger the setup — say, if there are a lot of cars involved, or perhaps there is more danger to somebody else — that's the toughest part. People watch all the time, especially young guys, and they say, 'I could've done that stunt.' And they could have; a lot of people could have. But to do it at three o'clock in the morning, with a director screaming at you and the car isn't half running — that's where timing, knowledge, and athleticism all come in."

Film producers choose southern Alberta partly because of the regional talent's expertise with horses. For example, the Japanese film *Heaven and Earth* was a massive undertaking. Eight hundred cavalry troops and three thousand foot soldiers prepared for one shot each day. "People started coming into the Morley arena at four o'clock in the morning," Tom explains, "and they'd start dressing battalions. By four in the afternoon, we'd be out on the battlefield getting all lined up and organized. We'd have one big charge, and that'd be it for the day. The next morning, at four in the morning, we'd start all over again. Those big battles were awesome."

Tom and nine other stuntmen were hired for special horse stunts. "We were supposed to be Japanese," Tom recalls, "so they dyed my blond hair black. When they wanted some action — somebody to fall a horse, crash, or fall off — they'd holler at one of us and we'd ride out. We banged and crashed for six weeks."

Falling a horse is one of the most challenging stunts the Glass family performs. Only special horses will commit to falling at a full run with a rider. Jason says, "Brent Woolsey owns a horse that will literally dive into the air and go down. She's very dangerous and hard to get down, but there are not many horses that will even do it."

The rare falling horses must be patiently trained, starting in a sandpit. "You first get the horse laying down," Jason explains, "so they're not scared of being on the ground. You hold their foot up, just tip them over, and feed them on the ground, so they can lay there without getting scared." The trainers progress to falling from a slow walk, a trot, and eventually a nice lope. "It's all command. You've got to get the horse past the point where they'll commit and do it — where they're comfortable."

When using a falling horse, horse trainers hire only certain riders to do the stunt. "You can wreck a horse in a hurry if you don't get it right and get it done," says Jason. "If you fight with the horse, and they won't go down, then you're beat. Then the horse has got it figured out, and you'll never get them down." To fall a horse correctly, he explains, "You've got to ride them right to the ground. A lot of guys will cheat and lift their leg out of the way when they fall. But you basically can't even do that, except at the last second. If you kick yourself out of the saddle and try to bail out, that horse will get right back on its feet and it won't go down. That's why falling a horse is a specialty. You're committed. You're going to hurt. You're going down as hard as the horse is. It's not an easy job falling a horse; they can easily land on you. It can take the wind out of you, or hurt you somehow or another."

To eject safely, the rider must bounce with the toppling horse. Tom describes the action: "The biggest thing is, when you hit the ground, go with it. If you start stiffening up, tightening up, or trying to protect yourself too much, that's when you get hurt. You've got to roll with it. Shift your weight, let the horse come down first, and then roll. Movement always saves you — don't hit solid. We've run down the sidewalk, got shot, hit the sidewalk, and rolled. As long as it's not a dead stop, it never hurts too much. That's the same with cars and horses: keep the momentum going and go for it."

Yet even when the Glasses are prepared, the horse falls remain hazardous. While performing one for the movie *Black Fox*, Tom recalls, "We were going wide open across the prairie, and supposedly a guy shot me with a rifle from across the ridge. My horse bailed in the air, jumped, and hit the ground hard. That was probably as hard as I've hit the ground. A week later I was still sore."

For another film, Tom doubled actor Christopher Reeve. In one day Tom executed a tough horse-fall and flipped a running wagon. "I hit a ramp and rolled the wagon, but then it was going to land on top of me, so I rolled down a hill. I hit the ground really hard." Tom shudders. "That was probably the worst I've been hurt doing stunts, but I never broke a bone. After that day, my whole body hurt for a week. Two hours later [after rolling the wagon], nothing had moved. It had just seized. There wasn't an arm or a leg that wanted to do anything."

The Glasses' ability to roll with the blow is also essential in fight scenes. In the early 1990s, Tom doubled for Richard Harris in the film *Unforgiven*. Harris played a blond Englishman who is harshly beaten by the sheriff, played by actor Gene Hackman. "Hackman beats him up," says Tom, "and kicks him and kicks him. It is a vicious, vicious fight.

"There were fifty actors, extras, and crew watching the fight, and I really sold out on that stunt. I hollered, took the punches, and grunted with them. The director, Clint Eastwood, walked down after the fight and asked, 'Are you okay?' I said, 'Yeah, I'm fine.' He laughed and said, 'You're the best actor I've got on this street. I thought you were hurt.' When you can fool the director that you took it hard, you've done a good job."

Tom attributes the success of that stunt to his acting partner. "Gene Hackman is such a professional; he's such a good actor. I was just amazed, because the next day my sides — where he had been kicking — were black and blue, but I wasn't hurt. The skin was bruised, but I didn't hurt internally. Hackman was picking me up with his boot. He made sure his toes were pointed down. As his boot came into my side, I moved and went with him. I took the kick before it actually hit hard."

Glass enhanced Richard Harris's character in the film, and *Unforgiven* was awarded an Oscar for best picture. Tom asserts, "The main thing with stunts is making the actor look good and not let anybody see that it is you. You hide your face and hide yourself coming into the camera — you've always got an arm up in front of your face. There are lots of little tricks."

As one of the world's best teamsters, Tom Glass is frequently hired for wagon stunts. In the late 1970s, he worked on the picture *Draw!* starring Kirk Douglas. "I was such a good double for Kirk Douglas that they could shoot straight at me." On the set, Tom recalls, "Kirk's wife actually came up from the back and tapped me on the shoulder. She asked me, 'Are we going for lunch, honey?' I turned around, and she was kind of embarrassed."

Tom's stunt involved jumping from a galloping saddle horse to the horses pulling a runaway stagecoach. Richard Cosgrave drove, hidden inside the stagecoach. To offer Tom handholds, rods were attached under the coach and straps were secured to the wagon pole. Tom explains the stunt's sequence: "I jumped and went down between the horses, and walked hand over hand underneath the stagecoach. All this time, the coach is running wide open. I climbed up the back of the coach, and then jumped back down onto the backs of the horses."

The stunt took a week to film with a helicopter and camera cars. "For close-ups they attached a Tyler mount on the outside of the helicopter and followed us. The chopper was overtop the stagecoach." Tom ended where he originally began: pulling the horses up. "It was supposed to be kind of a comedy — [Kirk Douglas's character] did the whole thing to get right back where he started."

The film *Draw!* is also notable for Iris's role as an actor. "I had a line. I was dressed all up as a shopper and I went to the store to get groceries. Mr. Horowitz owned the store — I'll never forget that name, ever. As I got vegetables out of the bins, I had to say, 'Goodnight, Mr. Horowitz.'" She laughs. "That was my famous line of the movie business."

In the early '90s, Tom's driving expertise was tested again in the film *Maverick*, starring Mel Gibson and James Garner. Lying horizontally, with only a peephole to see through, he had to race six horses to the lip of the Grand Canyon.

Several years earlier, while working on *Bird on a Wire* in Vancouver, Tom had met stuntman Mick Rogers. Rogers was hired for *Maverick* to perform a stagecoach-horse transfer as Mel Gibson's double. He was to leap from horse to horse as the coach charged towards a cliff thirteen hundred feet above the Colorado River. Mick informed the stunt coordinator that he would not do the stunt unless Tom Glass was driving the stagecoach. He was told, "We've got guys down here who can do it."

"I sent them newspaper clippings, pictures of my trophies, and articles showing that I was a World champion," Tom recalls. "Mick had to prove I was the best wagon driver in the world in order to get me to Arizona to work on the movie. It worked. Warner Brothers' lawyers spent two months getting me a temporary work permit."

When Tom arrived in Arizona, he was asked if he had driven many six-up teams. "I said, 'Oh yeah, lots of them.'" He confesses, "I'd never driven a six-up. I'd driven lots of fours, but there never was a reason to drive a six-up. But if they'll go, I can drive them."

Three teams of six black horses were used. "Some of the horses were grey, others roans, everything — but all eighteen horses were dyed coal-black." In the scene, the stagecoach driver dies, and Mel Gibson, James Garner, and Jodie Foster are trapped in the runaway coach. "For six weeks we shot the sequence across the desert. It was pretty wild. The six horses were running as hard as they could. Everything was a wide-open run."

Since the driver was supposed to be dead, Tom drove lying on his stomach inside the coach, underneath the seat. He looked through a small hole cut under the driver's seat. An American declared to Tom, "You can't drive six horses lying on your stomach."

"Let's test it," Tom countered. In the end, he explains, "It worked because the horses were running and I didn't have to steer too much — it was all straight ahead. The tricky part was running up to the cliff. We ran the horses up to within one hundred yards of the cliff, and then I'd turn them left. They had a camera across the gorge, shooting from the other side. As we got to the edge, we'd turn left and they'd cut it there.

"It got pretty exciting, especially for Mick Rogers, who rode in the front of the six horses. Mick was thirty yards closer to the cliff than me, and he stood right up on the front two horses, looking at the cliff." Tom did not try to stop the horses. "I just turned them, and made sure we got away from the cliff." He adds wisely, "We had run them an eighth of a mile before they got to the cliff, and most of the time the horses were ready to stop."

The Glasses' horsemanship skills opened the doors to other stunt specialties and opportunities. For example, in the 1980s, Tom worked as a transportation coordinator. "It was my job to move all the camera trucks, hire all the drivers, pick up the actors, take them to work, everything." He was transportation coordinator for the production *Stingray*, which featured a black 1968 Corvette Stingray. "For car chases, I bought fifteen old police cars from the Calgary police force and fifteen of our own cars. We'd practice with them after work. We'd slide them and skid them. That's really how we got into driving cars."

Following *Stingray*, the family seriously pursued car stunt work. "I bought an old yellow Malibu car," Tom says. "For two years, we'd practice around here in the country. I probably put six sets of brakes on it, and five sets of tires. We'd take it out, slide it, and skid it until the brakes wore out."

Reg is also skilled at handling a car. But, he says, "I learned how to drive by being a maniac when I was younger. I owned a '71 GTO. That was a wild, powerful car — the power got me out of trouble all the time."

While Jason was growing up, his family education included playing with cars at high speeds. "We've got an old paved road that goes to the gas plant. We'd rent cars or use Dad's old cars, and we'd take them out and train. We'd spin cars around or hit the ditch. I learned quite a bit of the car stuff from Dad and Reg."

Today the Glasses travel frequently to Vancouver to perform car stunts. In British Columbia, they have worked on *Millennium*, *Wiseguys*, *MacGyver*, *Outer Limits*, and *The Highlander*. "In the summer of 2000," Tom says, "there were fifty movies shot in Vancouver. We travel there a lot."

In car stunts, speed is the critical factor for both effect and safety. "Stunt guys say, 'Speed saves,'" explains Tom. "If you do a car slide or a car crash, speed will always save you. If you come in too slow and then figure you're not fast enough, how do you get up enough speed in a short distance? But if you come in *hot*, if you come in flying, you can always scrub it down. It's easier to get on the brakes and scrub it off than to get speed on the last minute."

Reg adds, "Everybody thinks you can cheat so much with the camera, but a lot of times in car chases, you have to be going twice as fast as it looks on TV. Rather than speed it up, the camera slows everything down."

Pipe-rolling a car is one of the Glasses' most spectacular stunts. Tom explains the action: "You put a pipe in the ground, angle it up, and hide it in a guardrail. At forty to forty-five miles per hour, you drive a car and aim for the pipe to go between one wheel and the centre of the hood. That tips it on its side. As the car goes up the pipe, it hits a 'kicker' — the end of the pipe is built straight up about six inches. It turns the car over — upside down. The car does a little twist and a half-circle, like a diver in the air. It comes down on its roof and skids down the highway. They are always a wild ride. It's just hit it and take what you get."

In the late 1990s, Tom received a phone call from Vancouver asking if he would pipe-roll a semi-trailer for the show *Road Rage*. "I drove an eighteen-wheeler to haul my horses around to wagon races, and I'm about the only guy in western Canada who does stunts with big trucks. I get pretty well all the work driving semi-trailers."

Tom discovered that nobody had ever pipe-rolled a semi-trailer. To ensure the stunt's success, he called his friend Mick Rogers. "Mick and I made sure the ramp was long enough [about forty-five feet], so that when the cab of the truck was going up in the air, the trailer was starting to tip, too." Tom and Mick also rigged the trailer internally. "We put about thirty thousand gallons of water up in the top right-hand corner of the trailer. We put the water in forty-five-gallon drums and strapped them in. When I began to tip, the water sloshed in the barrels and pulled the truck over."

For protection, Tom wore a helmet and the special effects department built a roll cage. "They used three- or four-inch steel pipe. In a car you'd probably use two-inch pipe." Tom was also strapped in with a five-point harness used in racing cars. The harness secured his shoulders, arms, and head.

As Tom was revving the motor, he says, "the adrenaline was flowing. You're vibrating. It's like coming into the barrels for the $50,000 [at the Calgary Stampede]. The blood is running so fast. It's no guts, no glory. Just take the hit." Eight cameras, including one in a helicopter, filmed the shot. "I figured I should hit the ramp at about 45 mph, but as I came in, I kicked 'er two more gears. I probably hit it at about 55 mph. That truck just flew straight in the air for about fifty feet before it came down on its side. It was pretty awesome," Tom reflects confidently. "It was actually fairly smooth."

Tom's nerve also earned him a job piloting a big grey dog down a long, steep hill. In the film *Incident at Deception Ridge*, Tom drove a Greyhound bus down a mountain. The stunt was shot near Squamish, British Columbia. "It was an eighth of a mile from the top of the mountain to the bottom. When we first decided to do it, there was still snow, so [the drop] looked wild, but it didn't look crazy. We prepped to do the stunt, and when we went back, all the snow had melted from the gorge. It was pretty near straight down, but we'd more or less committed to it by then."

The special effects crew installed a plastic windshield so that the trees could not smash into Tom. Three crash cameras were buried in the bus's path. "The crash cameras are put in a big metal box, so you can actually hit them and not hurt them. They were buried a foot and a half into the ground." Tom and the bus crashed down the mountainside. "It was so steep that the bus's nose dove and dug into the side of the mountain going down. It dug up all three cameras and threw them. There was over $100,000 damage to the cameras, and the bus cost $50,000. But they loved it. It was a rush."

Not every stunt's danger is determined by speed, power, or force. Most stunts are not dangerous at all. "Stunt work is fun," Reg says. "With 75 to 80 percent [of stunts], there's not much to it. In a car chase, for instance, you might not be one of the main cars in the chase. You might drive ahead fifty feet while somebody drives around you, and that's the end of your shot. The 20 percent is where you've got to take your lumps or scare the hell out of yourself."

Reg's 20 percent included a shot where he walked on a tightrope. "To make a bridge, we stretched a solitary rope out 140 feet above Lynn Canyon [in North Vancouver]. Two parallel ropes were handholds. It was an army training bridge. We were in full army gear, and we had to walk out on the rope. We're walking on this goddam wiggling rope, wearing new army boots, with a backpack and a rifle. There was no way to get back. Halfway out there we had to turn around. As the rope moved, you had to let go." He exclaims, "Talk about scarin' ya! If you fall off, you're lunch — you're not going to survive the fall. There was no safety rope, and we had to do it two different times."

Fear also comes with fangs and growls. Recalling his most traumatic stunt, Reg says, "It took place in Vancouver, for the TV series *Stingray.* I was one of the bad guys, robbing an armored car, and the good guys set a trap for us. They put a B.C. prison guard dog [a German shepherd] in the back of the armored car and I had to open the door." Reg wrapped four plastic soccer shin guards, two on each side, around his right arm. The dog's trainer told him, "If he comes at you, just feed him your padded arm."

"I opened the door and the dog just stood there. That was no good." The trainer told Reg, "You've got to tease him."

"So I tease this dog," Reg says, "and I get him mad at me — absolutely no doubt about it! So we get the shot."

Reg shudders. "The next shot is the dog jumping out. The trainer was beside me, standing just out of camera range. When the door opened, that dog came straight at me just as hard as he could. He chewed me up all around my groin." Needing stitches, Reg went to the nearby hospital.

When he returned, the stunt coordinator asked him, "How are you?"

Reg said, "I'm sore, but I'm all right."

The coordinator said, "Well, that's good, because we have to do it again."

"That dog still hated me," Reg states, "and I'd have paid anybody anything to have them open the back door of that goddam van." As he opened the door, the German shepherd again lunged at him, but he managed to stick his padded arm into the dog's jaws. Reg shakes his head. "That dog got a hold of my arm. You know, dogs eat bones. They've got strong jaws." The dog clamped onto Reg's arm and twisted his head powerfully. He recalls, "I guarantee that my arm was as thin as the bone. Jesus, he had unbelievable strength.

"We get that done, and in the next shot I take the dog by the collar and fall back, like he jumped me. So, the first time, I've got my arms stretched straight out, and they say, 'That's no good, you've got to get him closer.' And he still just hates me."

After he finished the shots, Reg says, "All the stunt guys came over and said, 'I don't know how you did that. I'd never have been able to open that goddam door again.' I said, 'Oh yes, you would. What choice have you got? You've got fifteen stunt guys watching to see how much jam you've got.' There's no way I could've backed away from it." He adds, "I never had a fear of dogs, but I definitely did after doing that stunt. I'm still more cautious now."

From underneath a dog to high in the sky, the Glasses' stunt work has gotten them into many strange predicaments. Jason Glass travelled to Mexico City to work on *Romeo and Juliet*, starring Leonardo DiCaprio. Jason worked on the film for three months. "The footage used was three minutes at that."

In one action sequence, Jason flew over the city hanging outside a helicopter, shooting a machine gun. Supported by one cable attached to his back, with his feet on the struts, Jason hung straight out horizontally. "It was kind of a rush deal. The helicopter was an old army model, and so the picks on the floor [holding the supportive cable] looked like rusted old bolts. That was the scariest thing. The whole time I was out there, I was just waiting for the picks to break."

Jason would have added more safety cables. "I just thought I'd be standing on the struts, so it wouldn't be a big deal. But as we got up there, the director kept saying, 'Lower him more and more.' So all of sudden all my weight is on this one cable. That was a pretty freaky time." He adds, "You never know what you'll get into some days. It always starts off pretty simple, and depending upon what the director's like, it can get a little hairy."

In the film *Rollerball*, a director's demands again tested Jason's athleticism and nerve. Jason and Brent Woolsey were chasing each other in Jeeps across the dark prairie near Lethbridge, Alberta. It was nighttime and they had no headlights; the filmmakers were using infrared cameras to record the action. "At the end of the scene," says Jason, "we came over an embankment, and she was steep! The Jeep was cabled off at about one hundred yards. And we had to jump out of the Jeep just before it came to the end of the pick. We couldn't see anything. We had to time it when the Jeep was going to come to the end of the cable and get out. We did that four or five times."

In the stunt industry, Jason is known for his horse work, but, he says, "Whenever you get a phone call to go to work, you never know what it's going to be. It makes it kind of fun." He has performed fight scenes, small burns (with his entire back on fire), and five-storey falls. One of Jason's most dicey falls involved jumping off a forty-foot-high roof, hitting a smaller ledge halfway down, and landing on piled cardboard boxes. "When you bounce off [the ledge], you never really know where that's going to send you. If you get lopsided in the air and land on a different part of your body than expected, it can shoot you off away." But Jason executed the stunt perfectly. "I came off, landed on my side on the little roof, just bounced, and landed right in the middle of the boxes. Sometimes you've just got to go for it and hope for the best."

Jason's sister, Corry, has been dubbed Canada's top stuntwoman. She lives in Vancouver and takes advantage of that city's busy film schedule."Corry is busy," Jason explains. "Only four or five girls in Vancouver work full-time, and she's got the right size and build to double a lot of the smaller, petite-type of actresses."

Stuntwomen must often endure more than the men, Jason continues. "The girls get beat up a lot more. Sometimes they only have a skimpy little shirt and a miniskirt on, so they can't hide any protective padding. They hit the ground and they feel it. I've seen a lot of women try to break into the movie business and go away. They think it's a lot easier than it is. They get beat up a couple of times and say, 'There's got to be something easier.'"

Because fewer women are available, Corry is sometimes contracted for a movie's entire film schedule. For Arnold Schwarzenegger's *The 6th Day*, Jason recounts, "She was on the set for about four months. Those are the good gigs. She's there 'just in case' the girl doesn't want to do something, can't fall down properly, or can't take a punch. Sometimes Corry's there for a week and doesn't do anything.

"That's part of the business — there's a lot of standing around waiting, not knowing. They try to follow a sequence of doing things day by day, but that gets changed. When I show up for work, I don't even ask now. I get there, go to my trailer, and hang out until they say, 'You're up.' Other than that, you'd go crazy wondering what the hell is going on."

As a father of stunt performers, Tom Glass says, "You get nervous for your kids, but I think I'm used to it, watching Jason drive a wagon. There is no more danger in doing the stunts than driving a wagon." Nevertheless, Tom's most unnerving stunts have included his daughter. "Every time I get in a semi," he explains, "they cast Corry as the girl jumping out of the way. We've done it three times. It's a little nerve-wracking when you're driving and your daughter is standing in the middle of the road."

In the first stunt Tom and Corry executed, she played a policewoman. Corry and her partner stood in the middle of the road behind a police car, firing their shotguns at Tom's moving semi. At the last minute, they jumped out of the way, and the truck slammed into the police car, dragging it down the road. Tom recollects, "As I'm heading down there, I'm sitting in the truck saying, 'Go! Go! Get out of there. *Corry*, get out of there!' And they stayed. And stayed. And stayed! Right at the last minute, they bailed, and I hit the car." He adds, "If I was the stunt coordinator, I would've been saying, 'Stay, stay, stay.' Corry stayed there right till the last second. I believe she knows how to do her job."

Corry must trust her timing, because Tom cannot stop the truck. "You rehearse it a few times and they pick a mark when they'll leave. But it's a gut feeling. Your gut tells you when it's time to leave. It's an instinct to save your life with. It's kind of eerie when it's your own kid out there, but she knows what she's doing."

As a concerned mother and grandmother, Iris Glass says, "I tell them not to bother telling me when they're doing really rough stuff. And they don't. Wagon racing is bad enough without having two things to worry about."

Trusting your instincts is a key element of stunt work. When performing a stunt, the Glasses emphasize that they do so without hesitation.

When stuntmen and stuntwomen overcalculate, injuries and accidents often occur. The job demands anticipation and youthful reflexes. "Instinctively, you will do things right," Reg Glass says. "If you start to plan how you're going to land or what you're going to do, that's when you really hit hard. But there's no doubt — as you get a little older, you lose the timing. You can't take the lumps without hurting a lot more than you do as a kid. I guess everybody runs into it. You think too much, rather than just doing it."

The Glasses do hit hard. In this job, the employees know they are going to be hurt. It is labor with lumps. And often the small, unspectacular stunts inflict the deepest pain. "The hardest thing to do, stuntwise," Reg explains, "is to do something three, four, or five times." If the lighting was not right or the cameraman missed the shot, then the scene must be repeated. He adds, "You first go out and everything's loose. You do your shoulder tuck and roll out of it. But after three or four times, you get sore in some places and start anticipating. It throws all your natural timing off. That's when it starts to really hurt.

"The saying in stunts is, 'Do it hard and do it good the first time.' You don't want to save everything for the next shot. When you blow in, do your thing, and the director says, 'We're over here now,' that's when you know you were a success. Get it quick. Get it once. Get out of there."

Reg repeatedly hurt himself in a stunt for the *Lonesome Dove* series. In the complete scene, Reg was thrown out of a bar, landing face first in the dirt. To capture his expressions, a camera was set on the ground near where his face would land. Standing on a step only six inches high, Reg had to fall straight into the camera. "I couldn't land on my hands. I couldn't brace myself on anything. I couldn't take the shock anywhere. I only fell six inches, but I had to hit the goddam ground like that about six times." Reg cushioned some of the blow with his elbows, but his chest absorbed most of the force. Two weeks after shooting, he was still sore. "Just think about putting your hands behind your back and falling. Even from six inches off the ground, it just beats the shit out of you.

"Everybody seems to get hurt on the easy stuff. On the big stunts, you've got all the possibilities figured out. The adrenaline helps to put you on your toes, and it's a great painkiller, too. If you're 'up' to do something, then you can do something and take some lumps. You don't feel the lumps until you come off the adrenaline."

Reg states casually, "Stunt work is like rodeoin'. You know going in you're going to get hurt a certain amount. As long you get up and walk away, you don't worry too much about it. You're just paying your dues with the smaller injuries."

Stunts are perceived as glamorous work. Yet the reality is far from the glitter and celebrity of Hollywood. Stuntmen and stuntwomen are anonymous players in the movie industry. "Most of the time, when you're doing stunt stuff," Reg explains, "it's *snap* — you're in there and out of there. It's a flash. Even if you do a big car crash, you might be on the screen for half a second and then the movie carries on. You have so little impact with what is going on. You just want to get in, earn your cheque, and get out of there."

He adds, "I don't tell most people what I do. It seems pretentious to me to say that I'm in stunts and the movies. I just say I work in the film business."

Jason also tries to downplay his occupation. "To me it's a job. We're behind the scenes. We stay in our trailers, come out, do our job, and the actors take all the credit for it." During the chuckwagon season, the media constantly quiz Jason about the movie business. "I always try to put it on the back burner. It's a good job, but it's just a side job. I'd rather stick to the wagon racing and the horses. We try to promote wagon racing. The movie business doesn't need any promoting."

Stunt work is punishing. Tom, who has absorbed many lumps and bruises, says, "Most of the day you're sore and hurt. I've never broken anything doing stunts, but I've sure been sore. Now I'm fifty years old, I think I'm paying for it. I've got aches and pains that I shouldn't have, [and it's] from taking crashes and hitting the ground. It all adds up. The doctor told me I'm like a twenty-year-old 4x4 Jeep that's never been on the highway — it's always been in the ditches. Pretty soon your body says, 'I'm not doing this anymore.'"

Using his experience, Tom has progressed into coordinating stunts and working as second unit director for such films as *Snow Day* and TNT's production of *The Virginian*. He plans to concentrate on managing stunts and letting younger bodies do the high flying and falling.

In the film *Snow Day*, Tom coordinated Jason jumping a snowmobile thirty feet into the air. Jason's cousin Chad Cosgrave sat behind him as the passenger. Jason recalls, "Chad couldn't see. There was nothing he could do but hang on. He smacked his head into the back of my helmet and broke his nose." Not wanting to cause a delay, Chad wiped the blood away and jumped back on for another three takes.

Reflecting on their involvement in the business, Reg says, "In *Snow Day*, I think the whole damn family was in it." Reg's fourteen-year-old son, Ron, had thirty seconds of screen time. "The guy running the rink puts on this Perry Como–style music, and it puts the kids to sleep. Ron supposedly falls asleep while he skates, goes straight ahead, and topples over the boards." He laughs, "He actually got more screen time in that picture than I have in the last one hundred movies."

In countless movies and commercials, the Glasses have been punched, thrown, and torched. But, from *Snow Day* to *Shanghai Noon*, stunt work has provided the Glasses with a comfortable living. "The movies have been a real good thing for the whole family," Reg admits. "We've done really well."

And, like wagon racing, stunts are a job that the Glasses do instinctively. "When it was fifteen below," says Reg, "my daughter, Riva, was out practicing stunts on her pony. She charged up to a snowdrift and pitched herself into the air. She did a big flip. She's kind of fearless."

"I looked out of the window," Iris recalls, "and Riva was lying on the ground. I ran out and said, 'Riva, did you fall off? Are you hurt?' Riva said, 'No, I'm stunting.' She jumped back on, takes another whirl around the yard, and away she goes. 'Oh my God,' I told her, 'you're going to break your arm.'"

Doggedly, the young Glasses continue to bounce and roll. They are practicing. They are learning. They are willing. They, too, will be providing anonymous moments of thrilling film action, entertaining audiences around the world.

12

The Grandest and the Greatest

It's in the barn where we survive.
It's our shelter. Our parties. Our home.
— IRIS GLASS

After four generations of wagon journeys, Iris Glass still eagerly awaits the green grass of summer. Time ticks by deliberately till she fuels her motorhome, straps Jason's and Colt's wagons on her trailer, and pulls past the Herefords onto the highway. Accompanied by her sister Kaye, she chases the wagon circuit. "Pulling two wagons, I put four thousand miles on my motorhome each summer. Nobody runs over me, because it is too big of an outfit."

Neighbors tell Iris, "Gosh, you're lucky. You go for one big holiday each summer." She retorts, "They should come with us just one time and see how much we holiday. We've got a lot of work to do. But we love it."

After seven decades, Iris's typical day at the Calgary Stampede remains unchanged. Her hours revolve around horses and races. "At 7:00 A.M. I get up, go to the barn, and turn on a big coffee pot in the tack room. We feed the horses their oats. Then we exercise the horses. I take two at a time, leading them around the barn four times. That takes about two hours." While Iris walks the horses, their stalls are cleaned and fresh bedding is put in. "We give them hay in the morning, oats at noon, and take all their feed away at about 3:00 P.M., five hours before the races." In addition to feeding the horses, Iris laughs, "I feed the guys breakfast and supper. They keep inviting others to eat, and ten will be sitting at the table instead of five.

"Usually, the afternoon is all yours. We go to the rodeo, the grounds, or the midway. At 5:00 P.M., it's time to get ready and all goosed up." Around 6:00 P.M., the Glass crew puts the saddles loosely on the outriding horses. Saddling the horses is a means of cowboy communication. "We get [the horses] so they know they're going to do something."

Iris has inspected the outriding horses for Ron, Tom, and now Jason. "I go through the saddles. I check to see if the stirrup strap is loose or broken, that the stirrups are okay, and I check up under the saddle to where the stirrup comes down, to see if it's solid. I always check every saddle. Even when the boys give me a hard time, I'll say, 'Just shut up and never mind. I'm checking it, too.'"

The outriding horses are taken to the infield corrals at 6:45 P.M. At that point the drivers begin harnessing the wagons. "We hitch the wheel team first," Iris says, "then the leaders. You always check, because sometimes a crosscheck gets over a line. The driver will tell us if a line is not done up right. Even when we're practicing at home, Jason will ask, 'Is everything done up?'" To guarantee there are no costly oversights, Jason double-checks the harness, ensuring that the snap on the lines is firm and the hames straps are tight. Iris adds, "You can have a horrible wreck if your lines aren't right. We're very cautious that way."

The Rangeland Derby begins at 8:00 P.M. During the wagon races, Iris passes the outriding horses from the chutes to the incoming outriders. "For forty years I have taken the outriding horses over to the corrals.

When the race comes up, I hand them over to the outriders. When the race is over, I take them from the outriders and take them back to the barn." After the races, Iris helps cool the sweat-lathered horses by walking them around the barns. She joins the circling parade of helpers from every wagon outfit leading hot horses. Iris then gives her horses a bath and puts them into their stalls with their hay and oats. Her work is over by about 10:30 or 11:00 P.M. — unless it rains.

Rain doubles the effort demanded by wagon families. "It's a terrible amount of work when it's muddy. You've got to wash the horses' feet even after the morning walk, because it can lead to infection. There is a crease behind the horse's hooves that we make sure it is brushed clean. We keep them really, really clean."

Tom concurs. "Those years when we got ten days of mud in Calgary — it was a huge job. The wagons are covered with mud, and they need to be washed before the mud dries. The harness is muddy, and it needs to be cleaned. The bridles, horse blankets, the shirts, jeans, all the outriders' clothes and your clothes — they all need to be cleaned, looked after, and ready to go again tomorrow. It's huge. You get up in the morning and do it all over again," he adds.

The enterprise of running wagons creates a communal camaraderie. The Glasses share in the chuckwagon *esprit de corps.* "All the wagon drivers are friends," Iris explains. "When somebody breaks down on the road, we'll stop and help, and when somebody needs a horse, somebody will lend them one. But when they pull into the barrels for a race, everybody is on their own. Their solid friendship ends right at the barrel. After the race, they'll go back to the barns and be friends again. It's a big happy family." But, Iris admits, "You get a little mad at some of them once in a while. There is a little tension, you betcha — kind of snarlin' now and then. And the guys get angry sometimes, too, but, like they say, it all comes out in the wash."

People who enter the wagon community often linger for years. Jason says, "That's the good thing about the sport — everyone seems to know each other. It always seems to be the same people around, year to year. And if a new person comes in — say, someone's new hired hand — they seem to be around for the next ten to twenty years. It seems to get into everyone's blood."

Together, the wagon clan protects each other. "At the rodeos, with all those kids running around," Iris emphasizes, "a child has never disappeared. The entire wagon family — three hundred people — watches over each other's children. The little kids are free, because their surrogate wagon parents watch over them."

Inside the barns, both children and adults play "chuckwagon." On the final night of the Calgary Stampede, the traditional wheelbarrow races are run. Jason explains: "It starts about midnight," Jason says. "Everyone gets a wheelbarrow. Some are stolen from wagon drivers who leave them out that night. Nowadays, everyone tries to lock them up, because they get wrecked. Basically, one guy gets in a wheelbarrow, and one or two guys push it. Anyone from twenty to forty years old does it. It gets a little dangerous — the wheelbarrows get going a hundred miles an hour with adults pushing and riding them, crashing and banging."

The wheelbarrow races are set up like typical wagon races, with beer cans as barrels. The one-wheeled wagons perform figure-eight turns and race around the barns."There's a hundred people sitting there," Jason adds, "watching and cheering people on. It gets pretty wild. It's a good thing it's only once a year," he laughs. "I've tried to stay out of it the last few years. I think you've got more of a chance to get hurt in that wheelbarrow than in a wagon." Jason asserts, "There is always someone trying to have fun one way or another, before or after a wagon race."

The Stampede barns have even been a marriage chapel, with the horses as part of the congregation. "In 1997," Iris remembers, "Norm Cuthbertson was married at the Calgary Stampede. The bride and groom came out and stood by the wagon. Everyone clapped, and all the horses in the barn whinnied. It was the cutest thing. I bet forty of them whinnied, and everybody roared laughing."

Laughter is a breeze that wafts constantly through the Glass barn. Purring barn cats are an audience in this musty theatre of jokes as chuckles and cheers rise above the melody of conversation. The barns and motorhomes are serious sources of fun and hilarity.

"Jason's dog, Utah [another black-and-white pet], doesn't like store-bought cookies," recalls Iris. "In Grande Prairie," she says, "we were out of homemade cookies, and I had some chocolate-chip cookies from the store. He was sitting outside, so I threw him one. He sniffed it, looked up at me, and gave me the dirtiest look. He reached down, picked up the cookie, took it across the road, and buried it in the shit pile." Iris roars. "We laughed all day."

The Glasses are celebrities in southern Alberta, particularly in Calgary. They epitomize the character of the region. Their family's passions are united with the heritage and culture of the community. And each July, when chuckwagons take centre stage, the Glasses are feted as part of wagon nobility. But, Iris says, "I'll never be a high-class, hootin'-tootin' celebrity. I have more fun just being me."

During the Calgary Stampede, she explains, "you can purdy near get away with anything if you've got a chuckwagon" — including driving her rig the wrong way down one-way downtown streets. "It's called the Greatest Outdoor Show on Earth, and that is as true as anything can ever be. All the things going [on] uptown are fabulous. You can go from 6:00 A.M. to midnight and never quit."

For years, Iris has participated in the pancake breakfasts, dances, and even stomping hat contests. "It's the Stampede spirit. It's atmosphere. Everybody who goes to the Stampede is happy — they're having fun, they're holidaying. The fairgrounds, the grounds are just sparkling. The feeling there is just fabulous. I just can't wait. It just shakes right through you."

After the evening's wagon races, there is always a party raging in the Glass barn. Their barn is "off the wagon." Iris emphasizes, "Some drivers don't like people in their barns, but we've always had quite a party in our barn. We like people to come. It gets so crowded you can hardly move the horses. We cool the horses, and when we come in the barn to put them away there are so many people you can't move. I always say, 'Hoot, toot — horses! Hoot, toot — horses!' Sponsors love it when you invite them into the barn."

Since 1993, Larry Shaw of Calgary's Shaw GMC Pontiac Buick dealership has sponsored Jason's wagon canvas at the Calgary Stampede. Shaw states, "The Glass family, like the Dorchesters, is what chuckwagon racing is all about. The family ties go back generations. And they have a consistency of being there, of developing winning teams, and carrying on from grandfather to grandson. It's been a pleasure to see Jason come into his own. He's right up there with the best of them, and on any given day he *is* the best out of them."

Shaw admits, "We initially started off in chuckwagon sponsorship thinking we were doing it strictly as a business deal. That only lasts until you get to know the people, and then you find you do most of it with your heart."

Larry has not been disappointed in his support of the Glasses. "In the Glass family, a thread runs through of being quality people — doing the right things, taking responsibility for your actions. It comes through to how they treat their horses. It's just there; it's the way things are done. I think you see Iris's hand in a lot of that."

A wall at the Shaw dealership is filled with framed Jason Glass posters, and, on a rotating schedule, a checkered chuckwagon is set up on the front lawn. Their successful relationship has been mutually supportive. Larry Shaw emphasizes, "I don't think they would ever let you down."

When a family member wins the Calgary Stampede or a World championship, it is a satisfying seal of approval. "It is such a payoff for the hard work the family, Dad, and the sponsors went through," Jason explains. "It all seems to make sense. You've been paid off for what you put into it."

Standing on Calgary's stage and receiving the bronze trophy, Iris says, is "the most wonderful feeling. The adrenaline is just a-jumping. It's so exciting. You know you really did something — something right to do all that."

Calgary's rules once stipulated that a driver had to win three times before being worthy of Charlie Biel's bronze chuckwagon trophy. When Ron earned the trophy in 1947, Iris recounts, "That was once in a lifetime you get to do that." The trophy now rests in Red Deer at the Alberta Sports Hall of Fame.

For the Glasses, 1988 was a year of especially meritorious performances. Tom was World champion, Jason was Most Improved Outrider (winning the Rod Glass Memorial Award), and Iris was Chuckwagon Person of the Year. At the World Professional Chuckwagon Association's annual banquet, Iris recounts, "They called it the Glassy Night."

Yet banquet chairs are not where Iris feels most comfortable. Her preferred seat is a cold metal bar. During the wagon races, Iris can be seen sitting on the infield's steel rodeo chutes, watching and cheering on her grandsons Colt, Chad, and Jason as they race. This is the throne of the "Queen of the Chucks." It is a well-worn seat from which she maintains a confident view.

"When these kids drive, I just never think about them getting hurt. Every time they hitch up, I wipe that right out of my mind. I say, 'Just start fast, go fast, and do your best.'" From her privileged perch, Iris has witnessed both success and calamity. "I saw Scotty Chapin killed, Rod Bullock, and Gordie Bridge. I saw them all run over and killed. Gordie was killed in Cheyenne, the same year as Rod."

When Bridge was taken to the Cheyenne hospital, Iris says, "At that time, after every show I phoned CFAC radio [in Calgary] and told them the results of the races. I did that for a long time. I phoned in from Cheyenne and said, 'Now, another wagon man is hurt. I want everybody up there to say a prayer for him.' I could do that. I just said to myself, 'You've got to be tough. You've got to talk about this. You've got to do this.' Not that I'm tough that way. I'm a real wimp. When it comes to my kids — boy, I'm a soft-hearted old girl.

"After Rod and Richard were hurt, if I let it get to me I couldn't go. Just as soon as they go to the track, I blank it out. I've got to do that every time they run. And if they do have a wagon wreck or tip over, you shake a little bit, but think, 'Not this time. They're going to be okay.' If I'm going to continue doing what I'm doing," she reflects, "I just have to think that they had a wonderful life as far as they were here. They were supposed to go, and that was it. You never forget them, ever. And you never forget what happened. But you can be at peace with it if you want to be, so I am. You can do it. I've always said the good times overtake the bad ones. When you do what we have in wagon racing, and as long as we have done it, there aren't too many bad times."

The Glass family ties are rawhide tough. On the farm and on the road, grandmother Iris and grandson Jason have a special relationship. "Jason and I are very, very close," Iris says. "He asks me all kinds of things. He asks, 'Now, Grandma, come on out and look at this horse's sore hoof.' He's always doing that, asking me to come and look at something."

Jason adds, "Since I've lived on the farm, she's probably been one of my best friends, for sure. It's over to Grandma's house in the morning for a visit. When we're away in Vancouver working on a movie, she makes sure the farm is maintained and the horses are fed, whether we've got hired hands doing it or whoever is still home. She's the one in the white house making sure things are done right."

Throughout the year, Iris offers advice built upon a lifetime of wagon experiences. "I still love it when the boys start to train. When they hit the barn door in the morning, I'm right there. I help catch the horses in the paddocks, tie them in, harness, and hitch up. I try to tell them lots of different things, like 'Your grandpa would do this,' or 'Your dad did this.' When they're breaking horses, I'll say, 'Now that little horse, he doesn't seem to like the lead.' I watch the horses. With Tom retired now, I've got to do more bossin'. Sometimes they listen, and sometimes they don't."

Iris is not one for misunderstandings or lack of conviction. Jason asserts, "My grandma says what she thinks. She doesn't hold back. If she sees something, she'll say it. She's always been the strong person that way. She's been around a million horses, so when she speaks, we listen . . . we try to."

In the barns, when a cowboy colleague offers a questionable tale, Jason says, "I'll look over at Grandma. Sometimes she won't even be listening.

She'll shake her head or she'll start a new story right on top of that story. Nothing shakes her anymore. She can't hear anything that she hasn't already heard or seen," Jason laughs. "She takes no shit from anybody. Nothing scares her or spooks her. She'll tell a story, and you'll wonder, 'Did that really happen?' You almost think she's got to run out of stories sooner or later. If something happens with a horse, she'll compare it to something that happened thirty years ago. Those kind of stories make a guy laugh, for sure."

At home, in training, or during racing season, Iris's wisdom and experience have been the family's foundation. "Grandma's always been the one that's there," Jason says. "None of us like to lose or have a bad race, but she's seen a million races and will just shake it off." He recalls one Stampede when both he and Tom were taking penalties and the week was falling apart. "Nothing would work. But Grandma said, 'It's one of those years. Next year could be the complete opposite.' She has helped me a ton by saying things like that and keeping a level head on us. She's always stable, whether you've had a bad race, a horse gets hurt, or whatever."

Iris is an inspiration to her family, says Jason. "We live in the country with a bunch of horses and we train animals. To me, it doesn't get any better. She reminds a guy of that quite often. She's very right. She's the backbone to what I've seen around here. One day I went to her," he continues, "and I went on about how I was depressed. Things were going bad." He chuckles. "She went up and down my hide six times, telling me, 'There's no such thing as being depressed when you're a twenty-year-old kid. You don't know what depression is! Just carry on.' I'll never forget it."

As she spurs on her grandsons' dreams, Iris dreads the day when she will be unable to assist or travel. "I would just hate to ever stop working with the horses, but I think I've slowed down quite a bit, too." Iris has broken both wrists, a finger, her jaw, and a shoulder, and her family tries to keep an eye on her. "The guys holler at me, 'Don't go near that horse!' I'll just say, 'Will you guys be quiet? I know what I'm doing. Now leave me alone.' Jason's the worst, but I just tell everybody, 'As long as I feel good and stay out of the way, I am going to keep doing exactly what I'm doing, until I can't do it anymore.'"

Iris's energy and enthusiasm for wagons continue to earn her daughter Tara's admiration. "It's really neat that Mom is very, very proud of it. It's been her whole life, and it still is. People can't imagine her going down the road in that big motorhome with the wagons behind, jumping on the outriding horses, taking them over to the guys, and helping hook up. She does everything. It's almost like she hasn't changed. She's done it for fifty years, and she's still doing it. She's always been there. She's the first one to say to the kids, 'Come on, get up on that horse. Learn to outride. Ride there in the seat with them. In a couple of years you could drive 'er.' There's never any hesitation of 'maybe you don't want to.' It's 'of course you're going to get in there!'"

After years of building a wagon-racing family, Iris still rushes to watch the next race. To her, the marvel of wagon racing has never been lost. It still pulses around the track, through her veins — through her being. "You'll never take the thrill out of wagon racing. I've seen thousands and thousands of races, and each and every race is a thrill. It never stops." She has no interest in pulling up. From start to finish, she is going to keep moving. When it is time to cash in her chips, Iris laughs, "I want somebody to run me over with a wagon, truck, or something. I never want to lie in bed. I've got to die really fast. That's the way I should go." Her sister Babe states, "When they made Iris, they broke the mould."

Iris is satisfied. She has no regrets. She is content, and she is proud. "I'd never want to live another life other than [the one] I've already lived. Never." She continues, "It's been the grandest and the greatest. I'm the happiest anyone could be, even with the tragedies. Sometimes the tragedies make you wonder 'Why?' but they say you can never ask why, because nobody will answer you. Nobody.

"So that's the way the world is, and you're not the only one. Things happen to others, too. Every day, round and round it goes. You get up every morning and live the best you can that day."

Encircled by black-and-white photographs of family and their horses, Iris Glass affirms, "I've had a wonderful life."

Glossary

Barrels: Two barrels distinguish each figure-eight chuckwagon-race pattern. Initially, actual wooden barrels were used. Now the barrels are made from a flexible plastic that can be molded and reshaped.

Barrel turn: The figure-eight turn each wagon makes at the beginning of the race. After completing the turn, the wagons make a counter-clockwise lap around the 5/8-mile oval track, racing to the finish line in front of the grandstand.

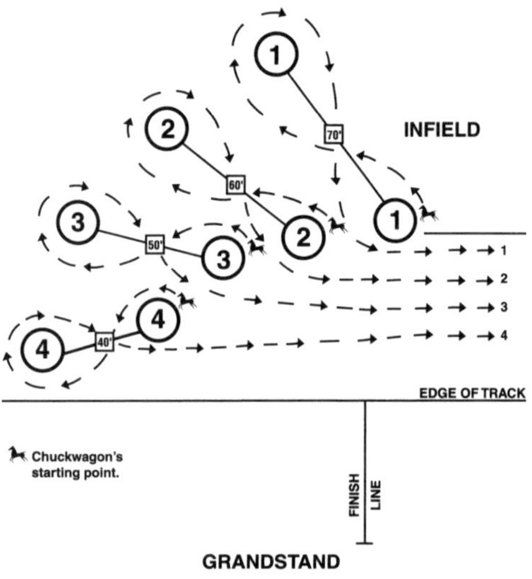

Barrel peg: The tent peg at the left side of the wagon, closest to the barrel at the race's start.

Barrel peg man: The outrider who has the job of throwing in the barrel peg.

Bridle: Part of the tack, or harness, that secures the bit in the horse's mouth.

Bucking the tiger: A term used in playing faro, a popular gambling card game in the Old West.

Canvas: The material covering the bows on the rear box of the wagon. The canvas carries the name of the wagon's driver and its sponsor. Also known as the tarp.

Chalk lines: Temporary lines drawn in the infield dirt to delineate wagon lanes.

Claiming race: A race in which any horse entered can be purchased by anyone who has made a bid or claim before the start of the race.

Crosscheck: See Lines.

Croup: The highest point on a horse's rump.

Dally: To wrap a rope around the saddle horn, often done to secure the rope after a cowboy has lassoed a calf or steer. Many cowboys have lost a thumb from a bad dally.

Day money: The prize money awarded to the outfit with the fastest time for one evening's races.

Doubletree: A pivoted three-foot-long bar bolted to the wagon pole. A singletree is attached to either end of the doubletree.

Dray: A low, strong cart without sides used for carrying heavy loads.

Fescue: Any of various grasses of the genus *Festuca*, often cultivated as pasturage.

Hames: The parts of a horse collar to which the traces are attached.

Hand: A unit of length equal to four inches, used to measure a horse's height from the ground to the top of its withers.

Horse opera: Early term for a Western motion picture.

Leader: One of the front pair of a four-horse team.

Lines: Long leather straps connected to the horse's bridle by dividing leather straps (cross-checks). The lines are the primary tool that chuckwagon drivers use to control their horses.

Long barrel: The inside starting barrel position. On the long barrel, the distance between the two barrels making up the figure-eight turn is the greatest.

Missed him out: In bareback and saddle bronc–riding competition, on the first jump out of the bucking chute, the contestant must have his heels in front of the points on a horse's shoulders. A rider who "misses him out" receives no score.

Oater: A Western movie.

Off-barrel peg: The tent peg on the right side of the wagon, farthest from the barrel at the race's start.

Outfit: The four horses hitched to the wagon. An outfit can also include the driver, the outriders, and the outriding horses.

Outrider: One of either two or four people who, along with the driver and horses, form a chuckwagon outfit. Each outrider is responsible for performing specific tasks at the beginning of the race, and for following the wagon on horseback to the finish line.

Peg man: One of the two outriders whose job it is at the start of the race to throw in one of the two tent pegs.

Pole: See Wagon pole.

Rangeland Derby: The Calgary Stampede's Rangeland Derby brings together thirty-six chuckwagon cowboys and their outfits. Presently, they include the four Stampede finalists from the previous year as well as the previous year's top sixteen drivers from both the World Professional Chuckwagon Association and the Canadian Professional Chuckwagon Association. It runs for ten days, usually starting the first Friday in July.

See the elephant: In the Old West, people who "saw the elephant" had found the mother-lode in their quest for fortune. Over the years the phrase broadened to include experiencing any thrilling aspect of the frontier.

Short barrel: Either Barrel 4 or Barrel 3, depending upon whether the race is among four or three chuckwagons. It is the outside starting barrel position. On the short barrel, the distance between the two barrels making up the figure-eight turn is the least.

Singletree: A two-foot-long piece of wood or metal, pivoted in the middle. The horse's tugs are attached to both ends of the singletree, and then its pivot point is attached to the end of the doubletree. Also called a whiffletree.

Stove: Originally a heavy ranch stove thrown by an outrider into the wagon's stove rack at the start of the race. Over time it was changed to a metal replica, and then a wooden one. It is now a light, rubber imitation that looks like two rubber pails joined together at their wide ends.

Straight start: A horse race that starts simply from a line drawn across the track. No barrel turns or starting gates are used.

Tarp: See Canvas.

Team: Two or more horses harnessed together to draw a wagon, plough, sled, etc.

Teamster: A person who drives a team for hauling or racing, often as an occupation. Now also used to refer to truck drivers.

Team roping: A timed rodeo event in which two mounted cowboys rope one steer. The "header" first ropes the steer's horns and pulls sharply left. The "heeler" then ropes the steer's back heels. Time is called when both horses turn to face each other, with the steer in the middle, ropes taut.

Tent peg: A five-and-a-half-foot-long wooden or metal pole, weighted at the top end. Two tent pegs — the barrel peg and the off-barrel peg — pull out and support the wagon's rear tent tarp. The tent pegs are tossed into the wagon by the outriders at the start of the race. Also called a tent pole.

Tongue: See Wagon pole.

Traces: Strong leather straps connecting the horse's hames to the singletree. They carry the bulk of the stress from the horse pulling the wagon. If the traces are not tight at the race's start, they can break as the horse lunges forward. Also called tugs.

Tugs: See Traces.

Wagon pole: The long wooden or metal shaft attached to the wagon's front axle. The wagon pole connects to the doubletrees and neck yolks. Also called the pole or tongue.

Wheeler: One of the rear pair of a four-horse team.

Whiffletree: See Singletree.

Wild-cow milking: A two-man event in which a mounted cowboy ropes a cow and the "mugger," the man on foot, takes hold of the cow's horn or neck. The mounted cowboy jumps off his horse and fills a milk bottle with the cow's milk. The first milker to run to the judge's stand with the designated amount of milk is the winner.

Wild horse race: Teams of three try to saddle an unbroken horse and ride him to a designated spot in the rodeo arena. The team includes the ear man, shank man, and rider. While the shank man steadies the horse with a long shank, the ear man subdues it by twisting its ear, and the rider saddles and rides the horse. All the teams compete at once.

Bibliography

Belanger, Art. *Chuckwagon Racing . . . Calgary Stampede's Half Mile of Hell!* Surrey, BC: Heritage House Publishing, 1983.

The Calgary Herald

The Calgary Sun

The Edmonton Journal

The Edmonton Sun

Gard, Robert E. *Johnny Chinook: Tall Tales and True from the Canadian West.* Toronto: Longmans, Green and Company, 1945.

Jennings, Kate F. *Remington and Russell and the Art of the American West.* New York: Smithmark, 1993.

The March West, July 1999.

Mikkelsen, Glen. *Never Holler Whoa!: The Cowboys of Chuckwagon Racing.* Toronto: Balmur Book Publishing, 2000.

Nelson, Doug. *Hotcakes to High Stakes: The Chuckwagon Story.* Calgary: Detselig Enterprises, 1993.

Savage, Candace. *Cowgirls.* Berkeley: Ten Speed Press, 1996.

Stone, Ted. *Cowboy Logic: The Wit & Wisdom of the West.* Calgary: Red Deer Press, 1996.

VIDEO RECORDINGS

The Long Road, Traditions — A Traditions Pictures Production, in association with CFCN and CFRN Television, 1993.

World of Horses with John Scott, Vol. 01, The Chuckwagon Horse, Kelowna: White Iron Productions, 1996.

AUDIO RECORDINGS

Cowboy Songs on Folkways. Compiled and annotated by Guy Logsdon. Washington: Smithsonian Folkways Recordings, 1991.

For information on the Glass family's chuckwagon race schedule, contact:
World Professional Chuckwagon Association
Phone (403) 236-2466 / Fax (403) 279-2247 / www.wpca.com

Young jockey Iris Glass sits astride Flame, one of her favourite racehorses. *(Glass family collection)*

Tom Glass acknowledges the crowd and introduces his outriders after winning the 1992 Calgary Stampede Rangeland Derby. *(Glass family collection)*

Iris Glass with Kirk Douglas on the set of *Draw!* *(Glass family collection)*

Tom Glass performs a falling horse stunt for the movie *Time Cop*, starring Jean-Claude Van Damme, as Jason Glass looks on, holding the Confederate flag. *(Glass family collection)*

Tom Glass in Jackie Chan's *Shanghai Noon.* *(Glass family collection)*

Corry Glass, Canada's top stuntwoman, in costume for *Shanghai Noon.* *(Glass family collection)*